In some ways, it was reassuring to have a big, tall, handsome bounty hun... bodyguard.

When she'd firs... hadn't known w... to expect. In the back of her mind, she might have been thinking she'd find herself a man who was nearly as spectacular as the landscape. A handsome cowboy with tight jeans and broad shoulders – a man like Trevor.

Last night, when she'd looked out her front window before going to bed, she saw him standing watch. In his shearling coat with his arms folded across his chest, he was the very archetype of a cowboy. Strong and silent. A man's man.

Still, an aura of danger surrounded Trevor that made her uneasy. She'd already allowed herself to be swept away by cowboy fantasies once. *Look how badly that turned out!*

There would be no more volatile cowboys in her life. Not now. Not ever.

Available in March 2007 from Mills & Boon Intrigue

Warrior Spirit

CASSIE MILES

MILLS & BOON®

INTRIGUE™

*First published in Great Britain 2007
Harlequin Mills & Boon Limited,
Eton House, 18-24 Paradise Road, Richmond, Surrey TW9 1SR*

© Harlequin Books S.A. 2005

*Special thanks and acknowledgement are given to Cassie Miles for
her contribution to the BIG SKY BOUNTY HUNTERS series.*

ISBN: 978 0 263 85697 2

46-0307

*Printed and bound in Spain
by Litografia Rosés S.A., Barcelona*

Here's to Thursday nights with the Vietnam
vets and the mariachis.

And, as always, to Rick.

CASSIE MILES

From the balcony of her Denver high rise, Cassie
Miles has a view of the gold dome of the Colorado
State Capitol and the front range of the Rockies.
If she could figure out a way to add the ocean,
she'd have the best of all possible worlds. Though a
typical day is all about writing and reading, there's
always time for a walk in the park or a longer trip to
the foothills for a hike or to watch the rock climbers
and para-sails.

Recently voted Writer of the Year by Rocky
Mountain Fiction Writers, Cassie attends critique
groups specialising in mystery and in romance, the
perfect balance for Intrigue. One of her daughters
once described her writing this way: "Romantic
suspense. You know, kiss-kiss, bang-bang." If only
it were that simple.

CAST OF CHARACTERS

Sierra Collins – Transplanted from Brooklyn to the wide-open spaces of Montana, Sierra was once engaged to Lyle Nelson, a lieutenant in the Montana Militia for a Free America. She has reason to hate the Militia, but will she betray them?

Trevor Blackhaw – The former Special Forces commando is legendary for his fierce interrogation tactics. What secrets will this half-Cherokee loner draw from Sierra?

Lyle Nelson – Though engaged to Sierra, there's no room in his cold heart for anything but the Militia.

Warden Craig Green – For years, the warden ran the inescapable Fortress Prison with an iron fist. He's days away from retirement.

Snake – So mean that nobody remembers his real name. Snake is the warden's favourite enforcer in the prison.

Boone Fowler – The leader of the Militia plots a horrible and spectacular act of terrorism.

Perry Johnson – Sadistic Militia lieutenant who wants to take slow revenge on Sierra.

Cameron Murphy – This highly decorated former Special Forces colonel is head of the Big Sky Bounty Hunters, determined to recapture the Militia after their jail break.

Prologue

Lyle Nelson strained against the shackles that chafed his skinny wrists and ankles. Under armed guard, he was being returned to the Fortress, the most impregnable penitentiary in the state of Montana. A hellhole.

White-hot rage burned inside his chest. The only way he could contain his fury was to remind himself that his stay at the Fortress was temporary. He'd be back outside. Soon. And he'd take bloody revenge on every soul who got in his way. It didn't matter who died. Cops. Feds. Women and children. They would all be sacrificed for the Militia's sacred cause.

The guards shoved him into a special isolation cell. No windows. Heavy iron bars. The walls were stone, and voices echoed.

Though Lyle knew it was cold in here, beads of sweat collected on his forehead and upper lip.

"I want to see the warden," he yelled. "And I want to see him now."

"You've got no right to make demands."

"Tell Warden Green that I'm here," Lyle snarled. "He'll see me."

The guard snapped his billy club against the bars. "Shut up."

If Lyle had been free, he'd strangle this moron guard with his bare hands. "Get the damn warden."

"I'm here." The warden strode across the concrete floor. "I want a close look at the man who thought he could break out of the Fortress and get away with it."

For a moment, Warden Craig Green stared into the flat blue eyes of Lyle Nelson, knowing that he was face-to-face with pure evil. The recapture of this fugitive was the worst possible thing that could happen to Green.

He turned away from the bars and gestured to the guards. "Leave me alone with him."

Grumbling, they filed out of the room.

Lyle stood close. His white-knuckled fingers clutched the iron bars. "I want out of here, Green."

"That's not going to happen." Only a few weeks ago, Green had arranged for all the imprisoned Militia to escape. He'd been well paid, but he couldn't take that sort of risk again. "I can't pull off another prison break."

"You've got no choice," Lyle hissed. "If you don't break me out, that cushy little retirement you've got planned is going to blow up in your face."

Green had been afraid of this threat. "You can't—"

"The hell I can't. I'll squeal. I'll tell everybody about your part in the escape."

"Okay, Lyle. Hang tight. I'll take care of you."

He turned on his heel and marched from the room. On the way back to his office, the warden made a detour through cell block A. As he passed the inmates, he paused outside the cell of a hulking, dark man. Nobody remembered his real name. They called him Snake because he was the most vicious and feared inmate in the Fortress.

Warden Green had a special relationship with Snake. They exchanged a nod.

THE NEXT MORNING, Green sat behind his desk in his office. He wasn't surprised when the door was flung open and one of the guards darted nervously inside. "Sir, we have a situation."

Calmly, Green asked, "What kind of situation?"

"It's Lyle Nelson, sir. We found him hanging inside his cell. He's dead."

Green lowered his head to hide the grin that curled the edges of his mouth. "Notify the coroner."

Chapter One

It was a beautiful day for a funeral.

At the edge of the pine forest overlooking the only cemetery in Ponderosa, Trevor Blackhaw reined in his dappled mustang stallion. He gazed into clear blue October skies. Beyond the western edge of the wide valley, distant peaks glistened with new snow, but the fields were dry. The wheat and alfalfa had been harvested.

Trevor heard the crunch of hooves on dry pine needles as Mike Clark expertly maneuvered through the old-growth forest. His sweet little gray mare nuzzled up beside Trevor's mustang. The stallion—a ladies' man—gave an appreciative snort.

"You gotta love this countryside," Clark said.

Trevor agreed. Though he'd grown up on the Snake River Plain in Idaho and was accustomed to spectacular scenery, he loved Montana. It felt more like home than anywhere else he'd lived, including the year he'd spent on the reservation in Oklahoma looking for his full-blooded Cherokee father. Trevor never met his father but was proud of his heritage. In spite of his blue eyes, his features showed his Cherokee ancestry, and he wore his black hair long.

He turned toward Clark. "The burial of Lyle Nelson doesn't deserve such beautiful weather."

"Damn right," Clark said. "That miserable worm should have been dumped with the garbage, left out in a cold ravine to be torn apart and eaten by the coyotes and grizzlies."

"Yeah?" Trevor tipped back the flat brim of his battered western hat. "Tell me how you really feel, Clark."

"Look at that crowd at Boot Hill Cemetery. It's not right that Nelson's funeral is a big event."

A couple of hundred yards from where Trevor and Clark watched on horseback, the black-clad mourners gathered around a pine casket. These were the people who sympathized with the terrorists who called themselves the Montana Militia for a Free America.

Standing outside the weathered picket fence encircling Boot Hill was a much larger contingent—the townspeople who hated the Militia. Some of them held signs. Others shouted insults.

And then there was the media. Swarms of them.

Anything to do with the Militia made headlines. For two months, the authorities had been chasing Militia fugitives who'd escaped from the Fortress penitentiary. They seemed uncatchable and had taken on an aura of ghostly infamy. None of them would be foolish enough to show up at the funeral.

"Let's get started." Clark flipped open a minireceiver no larger than a cell phone. Last night, they'd planted a listening device on the coffin. The transmission was excellent—good enough for them to hear the mourners clearing their throats and sighing. "What are they waiting for?"

"The preacher." From his saddlebag, Trevor took out a pair of high-definition binoculars and focused on a bald preacher wearing a long black overcoat. "I see him over by the parked cars. Looks like the preacher's giving an interview to CNN. Praise the Lord and pass the microphone."

Clark took out his own binoculars. "Tell me again what we're looking for."

"I'm not sure."

"Any specific individual? A signal?"

"We'll know when we see it," Trevor said. "We need a lead on our next bounty."

Trevor and Clark were members of Big Sky Bounty Hunters. Their job was to track down criminals and return them to justice. And they were very, very good at their work. All the bounty hunters were former Special Forces commandos, bonded in brotherhood and recruited by their leader to this new life in Montana. Each of them was well-trained in a specific field.

Their current bounty was the escaped MMFAFA. The payoff for each member was one hundred thousand dollars. Not that the money mattered. Trevor would have gladly apprehended these murderous bastards for free.

"There's another reporter coming over to the preacher," he said. "It's Kaitlyn Wilson."

That lovely little investigative reporter had shown herself to have a heart of steel in uncovering corruption at high levels.

"If Kaitlyn's here," Clark said, "Campbell can't be far behind."

They both scanned the crowd for a glimpse of bounty hunter Aidan Campbell, who had his hands full, trying to protect the headstrong Kaitlyn. Trevor had been surprised when Campbell, the extreme sportsman, had fallen hard for that female tornado. A man just couldn't predict where his heart might lead.

"I know what you're really here for," Clark said. "You're looking for somebody to interrogate."

"Whatever it takes to get the job done."

Clark cocked his head to look at Trevor. "Someday I'd like to observe one of your interrogations. To study your technique."

"Negative," Trevor said. "You don't want to know what goes on in the interrogation room."

Clark shrugged and looked away. "Probably not."

Even among the bounty hunters, Trevor had a reputation for ruthlessness. He was kind of a legend, recognized as the most effective interrogator ever to be trained by Special Services counterintelligence. When he went after information, he never came up empty-handed. Grimly, he said, "I should have had a chance to question Lyle Nelson."

"That supposed suicide was a little too convenient," Clark replied. "Too bad we can't get you clearance to interrogate Warden Craig Green."

Trevor scanned the mourners and focused on one woman. She was something special to look at. Sunlight glowed on the honey-blond highlights in her hair. She had dark eyebrows and high cheekbones. Even from this distance, her eyes seemed to flash with fiery intensity. Unlike the other mourners, she stood straight and proud, with her fists on her hips. Trevor adjusted his binoculars to check out her curves. Very nice.

"The blonde standing by the casket," he said. "Who is she?"

Clark took a moment to zoom in. "I don't know her name, but I'll tell you this. That is one angry woman."

Mike Clark had also been trained in strategic intelligence collection. His greatest talent was reading body language and subtle emotions. Trevor referred to him as "the human lie detector."

Trevor studied the blonde. "She doesn't look like she belongs here. Her black coat is something a city gal would wear."

"And it's a little shabby," Clark said. "Like she's fallen on hard times. Maybe that's why she's so mad."

The preacher finally made his way to the graveside. He opened his Bible. Through their transmitter, they heard his sonorous voice, quoting scripture.

The mourners removed their hats and bowed their heads…except for the blonde. Her full lips pinched tightly together, as if she were holding back a strong emotion.

"Something else about her," Clark said. "She's deeply unhappy. Doesn't want to show it, but she must have cared about Lyle Nelson."

"Sierra Collins." Trevor made the identification. "She fits the dossier profile for Nelson's ex-fiancée."

She'd be the perfect person for him to interrogate. For several months, she'd been privy to Nelson's secrets. According to one report, Nelson had contacted Sierra when he escaped from prison with the other fugitives. He might have told her his plans or indicated the whereabouts of the Militia's current hideout.

The mourners sang an off-key rendition of "Amazing Grace" as the coffin was lowered.

"…Ashes to ashes," the preacher intoned. "Dust to—"

Sierra interrupted. With her fingers clenched into fists, she strode to the edge of the grave.

A silence fell on the mourners as they waited to see what she'd do. Would she speak? Would she throw herself, weeping, into her ex-boyfriend's grave?

She spat on the coffin. Her voice came clearly through the transmitter. "You owed me, you miserable son of a bitch. Burn in hell!"

Trevor couldn't help but be impressed by her gall. "You were right, Clark. That's one troubled lady."

She'd said that Lyle owed her, which made Trevor think she might have been promised some kind of payoff. That made sense. He could only think of one reason why such a beautiful woman would hang around with the likes of Lyle Nelson: money. She was a girlfriend for hire—a tough, heartless woman who traded on her good looks to get what she wanted.

This time, however, it appeared that she'd made a miscalculation. Spitting on the coffin was a transgression that wouldn't be easily forgiven.

Three burly mourners grabbed Sierra Collins and forcibly escorted her through the cemetery, away from the grave. When a reporter tried to follow, one of the men snarled and the reporter backed off. They were headed for the road, where many vehicles were parked.

Trevor figured it wasn't going to be good news for Sierra when these guys got her alone. He tucked his binoculars into his saddlebag. "I'm going after them."

"Need help?"

"Three of them and one of me." Trevor liked those odds. "I don't think it's a problem."

"I know you can deal with three friends of the Militia," Clark said. "But can you handle that little spitfire?"

"I'll try."

He flicked his reins, and the mustang stallion emerged from the pine forest. Trevor urged his horse to a gallop at the edge of the trees. Smokey, the mustang, didn't need encouragement. This stallion liked to run hard and fast.

In minutes, they approached an outcropping of rocks and trees. Sierra and her three captors were hidden from the view of the people at the cemetery.

One of the men had his hand over her mouth.

Suddenly, he yanked his hand away. "She bit me! Damn you, Sierra."

"Let me go," she snarled. "Leave me alone, Danny."

"Can't do that," he said. "You insulted my friend, and you've got to pay."

Trevor rode up at full gallop. The mustang stopped short, and he dismounted in one fluid move. "What's the problem here?"

"None of your business," said the one she'd called Danny. "Ride on."

"You boys are friends of Lyle Nelson," Trevor said. It was a statement, not a question. "That means you're enemies of mine."

He sized them up. The one on the left was as tall as Trevor's six-foot-three-inch height, but he was skinny as a stick and pasty-faced. None of these guys was in good shape. Nor did they have Trevor's training in hand-to-hand combat.

Though he didn't take the impending battle

lightly, he was confident. His muscles tensed, and he focused his energy. Behind his eyelids, his mind became crystal clear.

He could take these guys.

Walking fast, he strode into their midst. There was one on his left, another on his right. Danny was still busy trying to subdue Sierra.

The guy on the left pulled a handgun from the waistband of his jeans. Big mistake.

With a swift kick, Trevor disarmed him. A chop to the throat brought him to his knees, gasping. His windpipe wasn't completely crushed because Trevor had aimed carefully and held back on his assault. He didn't want to kill these guys. Just to teach them a lesson.

The second man attacked from behind. Trevor snapped around, delivering a karate chop that broke his nose. The assailant fell back, moaning.

Danny released Sierra and made the tactical error of charging at Trevor. It took little more than a side step and pressure on the pain center at the elbow to direct Danny's clumsy charge into the nearby boulders. He crashed, then slid down the rock face, unconscious.

The other two staggered to their feet. Trevor motioned them toward him, but they both took off running, leaving the handgun behind.

Trevor picked up the gun. He searched Danny, and found another pistol. He stowed both weapons in his saddlebag.

The immediate threat was gone, but he didn't want

to hang around while the other two men recruited a mob to come after him.

Picking up his hat, Trevor dusted off the brim and approached Sierra.

"Nice job," she said. "Is that karate?"

"A type of karate. It's more like Korean street fighting."

She was even more attractive in person than when he'd observed her through the binoculars. Her thick hair was multicolored and tawny like the pelt of a cougar. Her eyes were dark. She held up one palm, signaling him to keep his distance.

"So," she said. "What am I supposed to do now? Should I tip you?"

Her voice had a New York accent. "Where are you from?" he asked.

"Brooklyn. And you know what? I can't give you a tip, after all. I'm broke. That scum-sucking Lyle left me without a dime."

"Money is important to you."

"Duh!"

He recalled his prior impression that she was a gold digger. But the label didn't quite fit. Her cotton blouse and black skirt were cheap—one step up from thrift shop. And the bangles she wore on her arm were junk. "I don't want your money. A simple thank-you is enough."

"Hey, I didn't ask for your help. I can take care of myself."

Trevor glanced toward Danny, who was sprawled against the rock, groaning. He was beginning to regain consciousness. "Before I got here, it looked like you weren't doing a real good job of protecting yourself."

Her chin lifted and her dark eyes flared. "I do okay."

"I want you to come with me, Sierra."

"How do you know my name?"

He shrugged. "You're Lyle Nelson's fiancée. That makes you famous."

"Ex-fiancée," she said coldly.

If she was sad about her former fiancé's death, she was hiding it well.

"There are a few questions I want to ask," he explained.

"Forget it," she said. "I don't even know you. What makes you think you can tell me—"

"You're coming with me." He shot her a hard-edged glare. "No point in arguing, Sierra. We can do this the easy way or the hard way."

Not in the least bit intimidated, she tossed her head and laughed. "Let me tell you something, mister. Nothing about me is easy."

He had the feeling that truer words were never spoken. Sierra wasn't going to cooperate with him in this interrogation.

On the ground, Danny had begun to recover.

Sierra walked past him and peeked around the edge of the granite outcropping. "Damn. It looks like there's a bunch of mourners headed this way."

"We need to get moving," Trevor said.

"Yeah, that sounds like a plan. How are we going to do that?"

"Ride with me."

Her full pink lips pursed as she considered his suggestion. "How do I know you're not going to carry me off someplace?"

"You don't," he said.

"But I sure as hell don't want to stay here." She glanced down at Danny, then looked back at Trevor. "Okay, mister. Let's ride."

When he boosted her into the saddle, her skirt rode all the way up, giving him a breathtaking view of her well-shaped calves and smooth, creamy thighs. He could have stood there all day, just looking. But they needed to make tracks. He mounted behind her.

His saddle wasn't meant to hold two people, and they were a tight fit. He reached around her to take the reins. "Hang on, Sierra."

"Wait a minute." She turned her head to look at him. "What's your name?"

"Trevor."

She gave a quick nod. "Okay, Trevor. Take me to my car. It's a peacock green Nissan at the edge of the parking area."

There wasn't time to argue with her. Danny was already on his feet.

"We'll double back," Trevor said.

With a flick of his reins and pressure from his

heels in the stirrups, he directed his stallion toward the north end of the valley. The headquarters for Big Sky Bounty Hunters was about twelve miles from here, and that was their destination.

With the extra weight on board, he didn't want his horse to be strained. But they needed to move fast. Trevor eased Smokey down the slight incline to the meadow. When he glanced over his shoulder, he saw seven or so mourners in pursuit. "Let's go, Smokey."

His horse broke into a steady gallop, easily outpacing the men who followed on foot. The animal was covering ground, flying across the meadow. But it wasn't a graceful ride.

And Sierra wasn't making it easier. She was wiggling around in the saddle. "Let me down."

"You're coming with me," Trevor said.

"The hell I am."

The pathway up the pine-covered hillside was narrow, and he'd slowed his stallion's pace. Before he could stop her, Sierra swung her leg over the pommel and slipped off the saddle. She fell to the ground with a loud shriek. So much for a subtle escape.

Trevor dismounted and stood over her. "I want you to answer some questions. That's all. Tell me the truth, and I'll take you wherever you want to go."

"No deal." Though she managed to stand up, her legs were shaky from the ride, and she braced herself against a tree trunk. "I'm not going anywhere with you."

When he reached for her arm, she hauled off and took a wild swing, which he easily deflected. Was she nuts? She'd just seen him take down three men. "It won't do you any good to fight me."

She swung again, and he caught hold of her wrist. They were face-to-face. She was breathing hard. Her lips parted and her face was flushed as she struggled to get free from his grasp.

Sensing that she was preparing to kick him, Trevor backed her up against the tree trunk and leaned against her so she wouldn't have room to slam her knee into his groin. "You'll answer my questions," he said.

"No!" Her head whipped back and forth in fierce denial.

"That makes me think you've got something to hide."

"I don't care what you think."

Trevor should have been annoyed. Sierra was making things more difficult than they needed to be. Instead, he found himself attracted to this hardcore, unrefined woman with the New York attitude. She was tough and strong and sexier than any woman had a right to be.

He peeled her away from the tree, spun her around, hoisted her off her feet and onto his shoulder. He strode toward his waiting mustang. The horse shook his head as if to warn Trevor that he was making a big mistake.

Sierra fought wildly, her arms and legs flailing. There was no way in hell that he'd get her back onto the saddle. Though he didn't want to get rough, she wasn't leaving him much choice.

"Last chance," Trevor said. "Are you going to cooperate?"

"Go to hell!"

He slipped her down to the ground in front of him. While she continued to strike out, he applied a choke-hold, and in a matter of seconds she was unconscious.

He lifted her limp body into his arms and gazed into her face. When she wasn't snarling insults, her features were amazingly feminine. Her mouth was delicate and pretty as a rosebud. Her thick dark lashes formed crescents above her high cheekbones.

She was a real beauty.

Trevor tore his gaze away. He needed to clear his mind, to focus on his mission. That meant he couldn't allow himself to be attracted to her. It was best if he dehumanized her in his mind.

Sierra Collins was nothing to him. Only a source of information. She was the subject of his next inter-rogation.

Chapter Two

Sierra awoke with a jolt. Her eyelids snapped open, and she blinked rapidly to bring her vision into focus. Where was she? How did she get here?

She was seated in a recliner chair with her feet up and her head resting against a pillowed back. It wasn't uncomfortable.

In front of her was a plain concrete wall. The paint was a drab color that matched the ceiling. On the wall to her left was a closed door. She craned her neck to see what was behind her. More concrete. This was a small windowless room—a prison cell without bars.

A shudder went through her as the walls seemed to tighten. She had to get out of here.

But when she tried to climb out of the recliner, she couldn't move. Her wrists were fastened to the arms of the chair. Her ankles were also restrained. Around her waist was a wide band that held her in place. What was going on? Why had she been brought to this place?

Her heart beat faster as she struggled against her bonds. My God, what was going to happen to her? Nothing good. That was for damn sure!

She pinched her lips together to keep from sobbing out loud, but when she closed her eyes, tears streaked from the corners of her eyes. There was a dull throb at the back of her head. Though she wasn't in terrible pain, she felt every single one of her recent bruises. And she remembered…

The funeral. Lyle's coffin. The men who'd grabbed her. And the one who'd rescued her from them. Trevor, his name was Trevor. He must have brought her here. Why? What did he want from her?

She heard the door opening, and looked up. It was him.

"You're awake," he said with a smile. "Good."

Sierra told herself to be strong. She couldn't let him see her fear and helplessness. Keeping the tremble from her voice, she said, "If you don't let me go right now, I'll scream."

"Go ahead." He shrugged. "The room is soundproof."

She opened her mouth to yell, then thought better of it. Her throat was too dry. By screaming, she'd only hurt herself, and she needed to marshal her strength. It was going to take every bit of her tough New York chutzpah to make it through this ordeal.

When she was growing up on the streets of Brooklyn, she'd done okay. Back then, she'd thought her life was rough. But the occasional mugging and street violence were nothing compared to what had happened after she moved to Montana. First Lyle. Now this.

She glared at Trevor. "Where am I?"

He stretched his arms wide to encompass the small space. "This is an interrogation room."

"Why am I here?"

"To be interrogated." He held a bottle of water in each hand. "You should have something to drink. You're probably dehydrated."

Though the water enticed her, she shook her head. "First, let me go."

"Ah, Sierra. I didn't go to all this trouble just to release you." He waggled the water bottle before her eyes. "Tell me about Lyle Nelson."

"There's nothing to tell. He's dead."

"When you were dating, did you meet his friends?"

"Yes." She eyed the water bottle. Her thirst was becoming unbearable.

"Give me some names," Trevor said.

"I don't have to tell you anything. Who the hell do you think you are?"

"I'm one of the good guys. And Lyle was..."

"Not good." She sucked on the inside of her cheeks, trying to get her saliva to flow. "And I don't believe you're a good person, either. You kidnapped me. You tied me up."

"Cooperate, Sierra."

"Let me go, Trevor."

"You remember my name. I like that."

As he came closer to the chair, his name wasn't the only thing she remembered. They had been riding together, crushed together in the saddle, she'd felt the sheer power emanating from him. What woman wouldn't be drawn to that?

Trevor had to be one of the sexiest men she'd ever seen. Tall and long-legged, his body was in prime physical condition. His shiny black hair hung straight to his shoulders. And his eyes…oh my God, his eyes were an intriguing, piercing blue.

She didn't want to be attracted to him. He'd captured her, dragged her off against her will and tied her to a chair. "You're a monster."

He reached behind the chair to place one of the water bottles on something she couldn't see. A table? A tray? Then he unscrewed the cap of the other and held it near her mouth. "Take a few sips. It'll help your headache."

"How do you know I have a headache?"

"Dehydration. Come on, Sierra. Make it easy on yourself."

She licked her lips. The inside of her mouth tasted like cotton. Though it went against her stubborn grain to do anything he said, she wasn't a fool. "Okay. I'll drink."

He helped her sip from the bottle. The first cool taste was pure nectar. She wanted more.

"Not too fast," he cautioned. "Just a little at a time."

When he supported her head with his other hand, she was surprised by the gentleness of his touch. She'd seen Trevor smack down three men with a couple of blows. And he'd rendered her unconscious with a tap on the shoulder. But he held her so tenderly now.

With a shake of her head, she derailed that train of thought. She'd have to be nuts to trust this man. At the moment, all she wanted was the water. She chugged half the contents of the bottle.

"That's better," he said. "You're comfortable, aren't you?"

"No," she snapped. "I need to stretch. To move around."

"First we'll have a talk."

She wiggled in the recliner, but there was really no point in fighting against the restraints. All she'd do was make herself weaker.

The way to get out of here was to be smarter than he was. She tried a different tactic. "I have to go to the bathroom."

He reached down beneath the chair and held up a plastic container. "Bedpan."

Did he really think she'd allow him to pull down her panties? As she gazed along the length of her body, she realized that she wasn't wearing her own clothing. She'd been dressed in cotton hospital scrubs. "You bastard!" In spite of her decision to stay calm, she jerked against the restraints. "You undressed me."

"This outfit is more comfortable," he said. "And I'm all about making you comfortable, Sierra. So you'll tell me what I want to know."

"Then you're wasting your time. I'm not telling you anything."

"You think you're tough."

"Damn straight. I'm from Brooklyn."

He gave her an altogether charming smile. This guy was really fine to look at. "Tell me about Brooklyn." His tone was courteous and encouraging. "Tell me about when you were growing up."

"You don't really want to know. You just want to get me talking, to loosen my tongue."

"That's very perceptive," he stated. "You're a smart person, aren't you?"

She didn't believe his compliment, couldn't allow herself to believe one word that fell from his sexy mouth. "I'm not telling you squat."

In the blink of an eye, Trevor's attitude changed. His lips curled in an angry sneer. His eyes were cold as blue ice. "You have no choice." His voice dropped to a low, dangerous growl. "You're helpless, completely dependent on me."

"I'm not scared of you."

"You should be."

"Yeah, yeah." It was taking all her willpower to keep up her tough facade. She had to think about something else, something outside this interrogation room.

"You should be afraid," Trevor repeated. His hand clamped hard around her throat. "The Militia are terrorists, murderers. If you know anything about them, give it up."

The pressure against her throat was just enough to make breathing difficult. She choked out the words. "I don't know anything."

He released his grasp but stayed close to her. His gaze bored into her face. "Tell me about Lyle."

"He's dead. There's nothing to tell."

Without a word, Trevor reached behind the back of the chair. He held a pair of thick cotton socks, which he placed on her feet.

"What are you doing?" she demanded.

He was silent as he fitted gloves on her hands.

"Stop it!" Panic crashed through her. What was going to happen? "Don't touch me."

His hands were rough as he slipped a blindfold over her head. She couldn't see anything. Her panic became terror. She was truly helpless.

"You'll tell me," he growled. "You'll tell me everything I want to know."

"Whatever you say. Take the blindfold off. Please."

"Silence," he said, "isn't always golden."

She felt him place something else on her head. Earphones. He fastened them tightly with a chin strap. She heard nothing but an unpleasant static noise.

She was blinded and deafened, unable to feel any-

thing with her hands. It seemed as if she were float-
ing in a terrifying space—endlessly falling and falling.

TREVOR STEPPED AWAY from the chair and watched as
she struggled. Maintaining the level of dispassion
necessary for interrogation was difficult. Usually, he
had no problem in turning off his emotions. Human
compassion was not an option when dealing with an
uncooperative subject.

But he kept thinking of her name. Sierra. Beautiful Sierra. Tough Sierra. Most women—or men, for
that matter—would have cracked when they realized
they were helpless. But she had put up a valiant fight.

Her struggling subsided, and he checked the silent
monitor behind the interrogation chair. The restraint
on her left wrist held a mechanism that measured her
pulse. The beating of her heart returned to a level
closer to normal. Deprived of sensory input, she was
in a state of suspension.

His technique was roughly based on the CIA
model for coercive interrogation. First came arrest
and detention. Taking away the clothing and any familiar objects was like stripping off armor. The subject became more vulnerable—more dependent upon
the interrogator.

When he questioned her, he alternated kindness
and cruelty to throw her off balance. The subject

should never know whether to expect a compliment or a slap in the face.

The next step was where they were right now. Sensory deprivation. The socks and gloves eliminated the sense of touch. The hood and earphones cut off sight and hearing. Without sensory stimulus, the subject became highly disoriented.

During Trevor's counterintelligence training, he'd undergone most of these procedures himself. Though it was intensely confusing to lose the use of your senses, the worst part for him was confinement. He hated to be enclosed.

In the chair, Sierra whimpered. The sound of her fear sliced through his stoic resolve. Though he reminded himself that the ultimate goal—catching the Militia—was worth her temporary discomfort, his heart didn't believe that rationalization. What he was doing to her felt wrong. He wanted to tear off the blindfold, unfasten her bonds and hold her in his arms.

He checked his wristwatch. In twenty minutes, the truth drug he'd administered in her water would take effect. Her defenses would be down, and she'd be ready to talk. The truth drug, or TD, never failed to produce the desired results. It had been developed in extensive tests with Army Intelligence and was more potent than Pentothal. Because the TD was mostly organic, with a mescaline base, the aftereffects were minimal, with only a few hours of slight, occasional hallucinations.

He appreciated the irony of using this derivative

from the peyote button, sacred to many Native American tribes, for such a high-tech application.

Her chest heaved as she sobbed.

Damn it! He couldn't stand seeing her suffer. This was almost more torturous for him than for her.

Trevor stepped outside the room into the hallway, closed the door and inhaled a deep breath. For this interrogation to continue, he needed to get control of his emotions. His response to her was all wrong. He couldn't be sympathetic.

Glad that nobody was around to see his weakness, he glanced down the hallway in the underground level of Big Sky Bounty Hunters headquarters. A quiet hum came from the room nearest the staircase, where they kept the computers and state-of-the-art equipment used for surveillance and tracking. This was the no-frills part of the building, nothing like the cozy upper floors, with their rustic pine paneling reminiscent of a hunting lodge.

Trevor had noticed that when he was doing interrogations, the other bounty hunters steered clear of this part of headquarters. Nobody liked to think about coercive techniques.

He checked his watch again. Ten more minutes. He had time to run upstairs and grab a sandwich, but he didn't much feel like eating.

Instead, he returned to the interrogation room and paced. Seven minutes left. Sierra's whimpers had stilled to an occasional moan. Five minutes.

There was no need for him to pity her. She wasn't an innocent little flower. This woman had lived with Lyle Nelson, a murderous bastard. She hung out with the Militia—heartless terrorists of the first order. Sierra couldn't be entirely blameless. Two minutes left.

Damn it, he couldn't wait any longer.

When he removed the earphones, she shuddered.

He pulled off the blindfold. Her dark eyes were wide, the pupils dilated. Her mouth twitched as if she couldn't decide whether to smile or to spit in his face. The drug had taken effect. She was ready.

Gently, he removed the gloves and caressed her cold fingers, encouraging circulation. "How are you feeling, Sierra?"

"Dizzy."

His first step was to get her talking, encourage her to open up. "But you're okay, aren't you?"

"Yes." She nodded slowly.

"Tell me about yourself," he said. "Tell me about going to school in Brooklyn."

"I was good at school," she said. "All A's and B's, and I went to Brooklyn College for a year until I couldn't afford it. Mom and Dad broke up for good, and I had to get my own apartment. New York is expensive."

Though her cooperative attitude was drug-induced, Trevor enjoyed this moment of civilized communication. With a damp cloth, he stroked her forehead and wiped the tearstains from her cheeks. "What did you do after you left college?"

"Lied about my age and got a job. I worked for a law firm near the World Trade Center. That was before 9-11."

"What kind of job?" He quickly directed her thoughts away from the tragedy of September eleventh. For now, he wanted her memories to be pleasant.

"Administrative assistant," she said. "That's a mouthful, huh?"

"Yes, it is."

"First I was a receptionist, but I got promoted. I had a bank account and savings, and I was even thinking about going to law school myself."

"What changed your mind?"

"Got bored," she said with a mischievous smile. "On the day I turned twenty-five, I realized that the farthest I'd ever been from Brooklyn was a friend's wedding in Philly. I wanted some adventure while I was still young. So I cashed in my savings, bought my Nissan and drove west."

"All the way to Montana," he said. "Long drive."

"But not far enough. I meant to keep going until I hit the High Sierras, because of my name, but I kind of ran out of gas." She tilted her head to one side and studied him. "You're cute, Trevor. If I took you back to Brooklyn with me, all the other girls would be jealous."

He smiled, enjoying her flirtation. The TD had

loosened her inhibitions as well as her tongue. "When you stopped in Montana, you met—"

"Where are you from, Trevor?"

"A potato farm in Idaho."

"No kidding! That's so…rural. Where else have you lived?"

"I spent a year on the Cherokee reservation in Oklahoma."

Her dark eyes widened. "You're Cherokee?"

"Part Cherokee."

"And I'll bet that's the part that doesn't have amazing blue eyes."

He couldn't allow this line of conversation to continue. She was a subject. This was an interrogation. "Now I live here in Montana. Like you. This is where you met Lyle Nelson."

Her sunny attitude faltered. "He was mean."

"There must have been good times," Trevor said encouragingly. "Tell me about the good times."

"No." Her lips pursed in an adorable pout. "Let's talk about the Cherokee reservation."

"Sierra." He snapped his fingers in front of her face. "Concentrate."

"I don't want to talk about Lyle."

And Trevor didn't want to push her. But this was his job. Extracting information could be as painful as yanking a molar, but they would both feel better when it was over. "Lyle's friends in the Militia. Tell me their names."

"Everybody knows them," she said, "from the newspapers."

It was time for Trevor to change gears. Niceness wasn't going to cut it with her. He held the blindfold so she could see it. "If you were blindfolded, you might be able to think more clearly."

"No." Her lower lip trembled. "Don't put that thing on me again."

"Talk, Sierra."

"Lyle's friends," she said quickly. "The leader of the Militia is Boone Fowler. He's a power-hungry creep. All of them are. Bad people. Lyle wasn't like them. He came from money, you know. He wasn't trash. But he gave all his money to Boone."

"Tell me about the others."

"The one I hated the most was Perry Johnson. He's nothing but a sadist, pure and simple. I saw him gutting a deer they'd shot for venison, and he was freakishly happy. Perry loved being up to his elbows in blood."

"Where were you when you saw him?"

"Perry's cabin," she said quickly.

That location was already known to the authorities. The cabin had been searched. "Where else? Where are they hiding now?"

"I don't know."

Trevor leaned closer, forcing her to concentrate on his face. "Did Lyle tell you any of his plans?"

"No. Nothing."

"When was the last time you saw him?"

"After the prison break," she said. "He came to my place. I rent half of a duplex on the outskirts of Ponderosa. I didn't want him there, but he wouldn't leave. He said he needed a safe house to lie low."

This was a new piece of information. After the prison break, the Militia seemed to disappear. Apparently, they had dispersed. "When Lyle showed up, why didn't you call the sheriff?"

"Lyle would have killed me." Her complexion paled. "And he would have killed the sheriff, too. I always wanted to think that Lyle was better than those other terrible men. But I was wrong."

Her voice cracked and her eyes welled up with tears.

"Sierra," Trevor called to her. "Concentrate. How long did Lyle stay at your house?"

"He came late at night, sneaked in through the window. He tried to seduce me, but I wouldn't let him get close. Then he locked me in the closet. I guess I was lucky that he didn't hit me."

"Did he hit you before? When you were his girlfriend?"

"Twice." The tears spilled down her cheeks. "After the first time, he apologized and seemed so sincere. He was under all this stress with the Militia. I forgave him. I was stupid. So damn stupid."

Her shoulders heaved and her breathing was ragged. Sierra's tough facade washed away in a tidal wave of tears.

Trevor felt himself melting toward her. How could he push her further? But he had to keep going. She had information she was holding back. Even through the tears, he could feel her resistance. "What is it, Sierra? What do you want to tell me?"

"I can't," she said. "It's too much. Leave me alone. Please."

He returned to the earlier topic. "After he locked you in the closet, what happened?"

"The next morning, I told him I had to go to work. I have two part-time jobs, and I can't call in sick."

"Did he let you leave?"

She shook her head. "I told him that if he wanted me to keep quiet, he'd have to kill me."

A gutsy move on her part. Trevor was impressed. "What happened?"

"He said he'd go. But before he did, he tore my place apart. He found my nest egg, the money I'd been saving so I could move back to Brooklyn. And he took all of it."

"Did he say where he was going?"

"No."

"Did you follow him?"

"No."

She was still holding something back. He could feel her resistance. Harshly, he snapped, "You're not telling me everything."

"No." Her eyes squeezed shut. She didn't want to divulge this secret.

"Why?" he demanded.

Helplessly, she shook her head from side to side.

"I don't get it, Sierra. You're a strong woman. You don't let people push you around. Why did you protect Lyle Nelson? Why did you stay with him?"

"Because he was the father of my child."

There was a hollow ring to her voice; she was speaking from the depths of unbearable sorrow.

Abruptly, she stopped crying. Her eyes opened wide, revealing her unassuageable pain. "I miscarried. After Lyle was arrested. I lost my baby. My son."

The color drained from her face. In a matter-of-fact voice, she said, "I wanted to die."

Her miscarriage was the secret she'd been hiding from him, and Trevor had forced the words from her. My God, what had he done?

She'd been right to call him a monster.

Chapter Three

Though Trevor's interrogation of Sierra Collins was complete, he did not unfasten her restraints. Not yet. If he released her while she was still under the influence of the mind-numbing truth drug, she'd be disoriented and confused, possibly even delusional. A few hours of recovery time was necessary.

He leaned over the chair and gently wiped the tears from her cheeks. "Hush now, Sierra. You can sleep."

"Don't want to." She gave a halfhearted tug at the restraints. "Let me out of here."

"Not yet."

"I've got things to do."

"Relax, Sierra. Relax." He keyed his voice to a soothing cadence. "You're tired, aren't you? Bone tired. Think about it. Feel how tired you are."

Though she made an effort to resist, her eyelids drooped. Sierra was in a highly suggestible state. Her defenses were gone, shattered by his interrogation. When she looked up at him, her deep brown eyes reflected a vulnerability that touched his heart and made him feel guilty. He had no right to strip away her dignity and pry into her life. Still, he asked, "Why did you stay here after Lyle was arrested? Why didn't you go home to your family, where they could take care of you?"

"Too tired." The words fell slowly from her full lips. "After my son died, I holed up in my house. Didn't work. Didn't do anything. Maxed out my credit cards. I was too miserable to live, and too scared to die."

It didn't take a psychologist to figure out that she'd been severely depressed. "Then what?"

"I don't know." She frowned. "One morning I got up and decided it was time for me to get a job. I've been working ever since. It's time for me to go back to Brooklyn, to forget about Montana."

Trevor would do what he could to spare her from the sorrow of her memories. Hypnotic suggestion would make her reawakening easier.

Gently, he said, "Breathe deeply."

Her chest rose and fell.

"That's good, Sierra. Inhale. Exhale. Feel the pain and stress flowing away from you. Listen to my voice."

Though she had no reason to trust him, Trevor had a natural talent for projecting his will. One of his instructors at Special Forces counterintelligence called it charisma. He offered her reassurance. "I'm not going to hurt you. I want to help you. Okay?"

"I suppose."

"I want you to think about a beautiful place. The mountains. Or the ocean. Maybe a tropical island."

"I'm from Brooklyn," she said. "I don't know from tropical islands."

"What's the most beautiful place you can think of? Somewhere special."

"The East River."

As she spoke, her eyes took on a less guarded expression, and he knew that she had begun to relax. "Okay, Sierra. Tell me about the East River."

"There's a park in Brooklyn where you can look across the river at the Manhattan skyline. And you can see the Statue of Liberty."

Most people chose a more secluded version of beauty, but he was coming to realize that she was unique. "Imagine you're there. Overhead is a beautiful sky."

"At sunset," she said. "The air is soft and pink. Then the city begins to light up. It's magical."

"Feel the breeze off the water. Hear the gulls and the lapping of the waves. Close your eyes and see it."

She nodded. Her lips formed a gentle smile.

"Now relax," he said. "Start with your toes and your feet. Allow those muscles to release. Now your calves. Your thighs."

"Feels good." A soft moan escaped her lips.

"Relax your hips and your buttocks."

Trevor glanced down at her full, sexy hips. Even in the shapeless garment, her hourglass figure enticed him. He longed to touch her, to hold her lush body against his.

This had to be the most unusual interrogation he'd ever done. He felt as if he was making love to her with his words, caressing her with his voice. "Feel your spine, Sierra. Relax each vertebra."

He could see the tension leaving her body as she relaxed her arms, shoulders and neck. Breathing deeply, she was on the verge of sleep when he whispered a final suggestion. "When you wake, you will remember nothing of this interrogation. You'll feel refreshed."

For a few more minutes, he sat and watched, making sure she was asleep. Her rosebud lips parted slightly, and the slight frown lines across her forehead smoothed. She was serene and so damn pretty that he could hardly believe it. Trevor whispered two words he had never before spoken to an interrogation subject. "I'm sorry."

LEAVING SIERRA TO SLEEP until the effects of the TD wore off, Trevor went upstairs to inform the others of the little he had learned from her.

It was unfortunate that she hadn't been able to provide him with a solid lead on the Montana Militia for a Free America—the group of homegrown terrorists that Lyle Nelson, Sierra's former fiancé, had belonged to.

When it came to traitors, the Militia were among the worst. They pretended to be fighting for a free America, while committing murder, sabotaging railroad trains and kidnapping innocent women and children. Their reign of terror had started five years ago, when the Militia had bombed a government building in an act of senseless terror that resulted in the deaths of two hundred people, including the sister of Cameron Murphy, the former Special Forces colonel who'd founded Big Sky Bounty Hunters.

With Murphy's help, the Militia had been caught, they were tried and convicted. They should have been rotting in Montana's Fortress prison, serving life sentences with no chance of parole. Instead, two months ago, they had done the impossible and escaped.

Though the bounty hunters had managed to thwart two of the Militia's deadly schemes, these bastards were still at large, and nobody had a clue as to their whereabouts.

It was damn frustrating. The Big Sky Bounty Hunters were highly trained experts who had served in the Special Forces under Cameron Murphy. They should have been able to nab the Militia without breaking a sweat. Instead, they were thwarted at every turn.

In the kitchen, Trevor ran into Mike Clark, who was making a sandwich. Clark studied Trevor, reading his emotions. Then he frowned. "The interrogation didn't go well."

Trevor gave a noncommittal shrug. He sure as hell wasn't going to talk about his attraction to Sierra. "Did you learn anything else at Lyle Nelson's funeral?"

"Most of the townspeople hate the Militia, but there's a growing faction of sympathizers. A backlash. It's mostly young men who think there's something cool about being an outlaw."

Disgusted, Trevor said, "The Militia isn't like Butch Cassidy and the Sundance Kid. They're cold-blooded killers."

"Terrorists." Mike held up his sandwich. "Hungry?"

"Not now. Is Murphy around?"

"In the front."

Trevor entered the large, pine-paneled room where Tony Lombardi and Jacob Powell were playing darts. Lombardi scored at the edge of the bull's-eye and broke into a victory dance. In his Bronx accent, he chanted, "Oh, yeah. I'm the champ. Oh, yeah."

"You? Beating me?" Powell scoffed. "No way do I lose to a geologist."

"You know what they say—Geologists got stones."

Powell's eyes narrowed as he took aim, then flipped his dart. Dead center. "The champ? You're the chump."

"How'd you do that?"

Powell—a decorated fighter pilot and aviator—

pointed to his green eyes, then flared his fingers. "Eye-hand coordination. I'm the best. That's why you can call me Bull's-eye Powell."

Lombardi rolled his eyes. "That's some bull, all right."

"Admit it. I beat your sorry ass."

"Hey! This is a fine ass," Lombardi protested. "Ask any female."

He used his geology training in tracking, but Lombardi's real talent was finding ladies who were susceptible to his charms. "Maybe you guys should come with me tonight. There's this little tavern in Helena where the beer is cold and the ladies are hot."

"Isabella wouldn't like that." Powell couldn't help grinning as he said the name of the woman he loved.

"She's got you on a leash," Lombardi teased.

"There's no place else I want to be," his friend admitted.

Lombardi groaned and turned to Trevor. "You want to come to Helena tonight?"

"I'm busy." He needed to wait a couple of hours before taking Sierra home. After that, he wanted to keep his options open in case she needed more assistance.

Cameron Murphy, who was sitting in a rocking chair near the window, interrupted. "Blackhaw, what did you learn from the subject?"

Though they were no longer in the military, Trevor had the feeling that he should snap to attention. He respected his former commanding officer more than any man alive.

"Sierra Collins," he said. "Formerly engaged to Lyle Nelson. She hates the Militia. And Lyle. He stole the money she'd been saving to move back to Brooklyn."

"She's a Brooklyn babe," Lombardi said with a knowing grin. "Smart. Tight-lipped. Tough. How the hell did she end up in Montana?"

"She's wondering the same thing," Trevor replied.

"Any information," Murphy asked, "about the Militia's hideout?"

"No. But after the jailbreak, Lyle returned to her house for one night. Our prior assumption that the Militia stuck together was incorrect."

"Hold it," Lombardi said. In an instant, his smart-aleck attitude transformed to seriousness. "My analysis of the soil samples from Lyle Nelson's boots led us to the deserted copper mine. That's where they stayed after the jailbreak."

"After that," Trevor said, "they dispersed. Lyle Nelson went to Sierra's house."

"If she hates him so much," Lombardi asked, "why didn't she turn him in?"

"She was in a hostage situation," Trevor said.

"Do you believe her?" Murphy probed.

"She wasn't holding anything back." Trevor vividly recalled the agony she'd gone through in revealing her most closely held secret, about her miscarriage. "She doesn't know where the Militia is hiding out."

"Nonetheless," Murphy said, "Sierra Collins might be of value to us."

"How so?"

"If she hates the Militia as much as she claims, they might feel the same way about her."

"Are you suggesting they might come after her?"

"Revenge," Murphy stated. "It's part of the Militia's creed."

"I agree," Clark said as he joined them. "Sierra didn't make any friends at the funeral when she spat on Lyle Nelson's coffin and said he should burn in hell."

"That took nerve," Lombardi murmured. "She's a Brooklyn babe, for sure."

Trevor hadn't been thinking of Sierra as a potential victim, but it was a strong possibility. If the Militia wanted to teach her a lesson… "Damn it!"

"Problem?" Murphy asked.

"I might have made her situation worse. I might have antagonized a couple of sympathizers at the funeral."

"Might have?"

"Three men threatened her," Trevor said. "I took them down."

"Geez," Lombardi said. "Good way to keep a low profile, Blackhaw."

Though the bounty hunters didn't go out of their way

to keep their identities secret, they didn't advertise their presence. Outside of law enforcement, most people weren't aware of their existence as an organized group.

"I'll keep an eye on Sierra," Trevor said. "If the Militia comes after her, I'll be ready for them."

Murphy nodded. "That's as good a plan as any. Those snakes have gone underground, and we're not having much luck in finding their den."

Powell went to the board and gathered his darts. He grumbled, "This should have been over. The Militia isn't smart enough to keep evading us."

"Don't underestimate them," Murphy warned. "We're not the only ones in the dark. State and national law enforcement are also involved."

"Don't I know it," Powell said. His beloved Isabella was Secret Service. "I think there's somebody else working with the Militia, pulling their strings. Somebody has got to be financing them."

Though the other men nodded in agreement, Trevor's mind was elsewhere. He'd heard all these arguments before and agreed with them. The Militia might have started out working alone, but it seemed they could now be part of a larger terrorist campaign.

His thoughts returned to Sierra. How could a single, innocent woman hope to stand up to the Militia, much less to a greater force of evil? Her actions at the funeral had been gutsy, but not wise. It would be his job to protect her now.

While the other men made plans and divided up

duties, Trevor returned to the basement interrogation room, where Sierra still slept peacefully as a tawny kitten with a full belly of sweet cream. This kitten had claws, he reminded himself. When it came to defending herself, she was more like a tiger cub than a domesticated tabby cat.

Carefully, he unfastened the restraints on her arms, legs and waist. With light strokes, he massaged her hands to encourage circulation. Though the skin above her wrist was soft and pale, her palms were callused from hard work. She'd mentioned that she had two jobs. Where? What kind of work?

Trevor frowned. Sierra had an active schedule. Keeping an eye on her was going to be difficult unless he could convince her to invite him into her life, to let him get close . . . but not too close. He needed to maintain emotional distance. Getting personally involved with her would be a mistake.

Yet as he settled down to watch patiently while she slept, his heart stirred. She was different. She touched him in ways no one had before.

SIERRA WAS STUCK in a nightmare—aware that she was dreaming but unable to wake. Surrounded by thick fog, she spun around and saw Lyle stalking toward her. This was only a dream. Not real. Lyle was dead and buried. He could never hurt her again. Yet he reached out with long skeletal fingers.

His face was horrible. His eyes bulged from their

sockets. His chin hung slack, and there were purple bruises around his neck. They said he'd hanged himself in his prison cell, but she didn't believe it. Lyle was too mean to commit suicide.

His jaw creaked open. He spoke. "Sierra, find my killer. You owe me that much."

"I don't," she protested. "I don't owe you squat."

She started running. Her feet were numb. She could hardly move. But she couldn't let Lyle touch her and pull her into the grave with him.

She ran as fast as she could, into the trees. The forest closed around her. Then she saw another man, tall and still. His long black hair fell to his shoulders. His startling blue eyes drew her toward him. "Trevor," she whispered.

His arms enfolded her. This felt so real; she could hear his heart beating, could smell his masculine scent. Her fingernails scratched against the cotton of his shirt. When she looked up at him, she was amazed by how handsome he was—his high cheekbones and straight nose. And his lips…

She wanted to kiss those well-shaped lips. Well, why not? She could hardly blame herself for dreaming. "Kiss me, Trevor."

His mouth joined with hers. An incredible warmth flowed through her veins. Oh God, this was good. It seemed right. She felt alive and strong.

His mouth moved against hers, and she darted her

tongue across the surface of his lips. He responded with the skill and strength she had come to expect from him after knowing him for only a few short hours. Pure sensation washed over her. This kiss was sexier than anything she'd felt before, sexier than going all the way with most men.

With a sigh, she separated from him. Awash in pleasure, she leaned back and enjoyed the fantastic awakening of her sensuality. "Oh, Trevor."

She lifted her hand to her tingling lips. So good. So very good.

Then Sierra opened her eyes and blinked. Trevor was nowhere in sight. She was alone in the square, featureless room. Her arms were no longer tied down, and she raised her hands to her face. Her cheeks felt warm, probably because of her sensual dream. Or something else? What was it? Though she was refreshed and alert, her mind was blank, as though recent memories had been swept clean.

She knew that Trevor had brought her to this place. He had tied her up and asked her questions, and she remembered feeling angry and sad. But why? "Lyle," she said.

Sierra pushed herself out of the chair, went to the door and twisted the handle. Trevor stood in the hallway outside. He nodded to her.

He was as gorgeous as in her dream. Tall and lean and muscular. His black hair, pulled back in a ponytail, glistened. And those blue, blue eyes!

But he wasn't her fantasy lover. This man was her captor, and she hated his guts. "I want to go home."

"Sure thing," he said. "Come with me."

She followed him down the hallway. They seemed to be in a basement with low ceilings, but there wasn't a musty smell. This place was clean, almost sterile. "Where are we?"

Instead of answering, Trevor pushed open the door to a bathroom. "Your clothes are inside if you want to change."

Though she had a million questions, Sierra also had an overwhelming urge to pee. Bathroom first. Questions later.

She relieved her bladder, dressed quickly and splashed water on her face. When she slipped on her wristwatch, she noted that it was after six o'clock. She'd been here almost four hours. Doing what? She hadn't been sleeping all that time.

Her purse sat on the counter beside the sink, and she checked the contents. Her lipstick, breath mints and ball-point pen were there. She still had seven dollars in her wallet. The only thing missing was her precise memory of what had happened to her in that interrogation room.

She returned to the hallway, where Trevor was waiting.

"How are you feeling?" he asked.

"I've been better." She braced her fists on her hips. "Now I have some questions for you."

"Shoot."

"Let's start with this—where the hell are we?"

"A good-size cabin with a couple of outbuildings, a barn and a stable in back. It belongs to Cameron Murphy."

The name sounded familiar, but she couldn't put a face with it. "Why did you bring me here?"

"I thought you might have information." He placed his battered black cowboy hat on his head and started down the hallway at a casual saunter. "I expect you're ready to get home."

She also wanted answers. And he was being deliberately evasive. "Hold it right there, Trevor."

Raising one eyebrow, he gave her a look that was about as innocent as that of a mountain lion. "Is there a problem?"

"Damn right! You threw me on your horse, brought me here and tied me up in that weird little room. I want to know why."

"I asked you some questions." He smiled calmly, but she remembered his other expression. His shimmering blue eyes could also be hard and angry. He was capable of inspiring fear. And yet when she'd dreamed about that kiss he'd been something else altogether.

"Who are you?" she asked. "What's your job?"

"I'm a bounty hunter."

"And you're after the Militia." When he opened the door to a root cellar, she balked. "Where are you taking me?"

"This is a back door. I wanted to avoid anybody who might be upstairs."

Still she hesitated to follow him. "I don't trust you."

"I won't hurt you, Sierra. You have my word."

"The word of a bounty hunter? That's not reassuring."

"We're on the same side," he said. "You and I want the same thing."

"To bring down the Militia?"

"You hate them as much as I do. Probably more."

"But I'm not going after them." She wanted to be left alone, to get on with her life. "I want no part of them. Or of you."

"Will you allow me to take you home?"

She gave a curt nod. "And that will be the last we'll ever see of each other."

As she followed him to the doorway and out into the night, her firm decision wavered. Seeing Trevor again might not be the worst thing that ever happened to her.

Chapter Four

In the hour of darkness just before dawn, Boone Fowler left the rough-hewn bunkhouse that currently housed the Montana Militia for a Free America. No matter what anybody said, he'd done a damn good job as their leader. Taking possession of this long, one-story structure attached to an empty barn and corral had been a stroke of genius. The bunkhouse—deserted years ago by a rancher who went out of business—made a perfect hideout. The location was remote, accessible only by one dirt road that was easily guarded.

When Boone and his men moved in, they'd repaired the cracks in the walls and blacked out the windows. They'd installed a high-tech, silent generator so there would be no telltale wisps of smoke rising from the chimney. Nobody, by God, could find them.

The problem with the hideout was the enforced and constant proximity. Boone and his men slept, cooked and ate in the same long room. Aware of aerial surveillance by those who were after them, the Militiamen limited their daytime exposure.

If they were vigilant, they wouldn't be caught. But safety wasn't Boone Fowler's deepest concern on this cold October morning. He had a plan—a detailed scheme that would require full cooperation from his men. And he was concerned about Perry Johnson, who had recently shown himself to be a wild card.

Boone's step was stealthy as he entered the forested terrain behind the bunkhouse. The carpet of pine needles beneath his boots hardly made a whisper. He touched the handle of the automatic pistol in his pocket. Though he hated to lose Perry, disloyalty could not be tolerated. The Militia had a greater cause and no one could stand in the way. Not even Perry.

The first glimmer of sunrise filtered through the conifer branches and the rust-colored autumn leaves on the chokecherry bushes. A damp, bone-chilling mist rose from the earth. A weaker man would have shivered. Not Boone. He drew strength from natural adversity. These mountains were his goddamn birthright as an American. This time, he would prevail, surviving against the will of the combined state and federal law enforcement stooges. He would send a clear and brutal message. And they would listen. This time, the Militia would not be apprehended.

At the edge of a creek, Boone spotted two men hunkered down by the stream fishing for breakfast trout. Instead of approaching them, he hung back to listen, and drew his gun.

Raymond Fleming, a scrawny beanpole, sounded angry. "We can't keep hiding out. People are going to think we gave up."

"And what the hell do you think we ought to do?" Perry Johnson tugged on his fishing line. "Paint targets on our foreheads and march into Ponderosa?"

"I don't know." Raymond shrugged his skinny shoulders. "Something."

"That's a hell of a plan," Perry scoffed. "You're not exactly the sharpest arrow in the quiver, are you?"

"Hey, it's not even morning yet. My brain isn't awake." Raymond fidgeted. "And I'm not the one who was stupid enough to sneak off and go to Lyle's funeral. That was you, Perry."

Without dropping his fishing pole, Perry lashed out. His bare fist snapped against Raymond's temple, sending the younger man sprawling.

"Hey!" Raymond shouted. "What was that for?"

"Calling me stupid."

Perry rose to his feet. His burly shoulders flared as he looked down at Raymond. In the glow of sunrise, Boone watched the impressive transformation of Perry Johnson from fisherman to predator. He was a dangerous man. Ruthless. It would be a shame to kill him.

Raymond cowered. "I didn't mean it like that. I'd never call you dumb. Hell, sometimes I even think you're smarter than Boone. It's just that somebody could have recognized you at the funeral."

"But they didn't." Still holding his rod, Perry used his other hand to remove his cap and rub the sleeve of his jacket across his bald forehead. Then he replaced the cap. Back in control again. "Damn near broke my heart to see what happened at Lyle's grave. A bunch of media jackasses crawling all over, showing no respect. And that little bitch, Sierra. She spat on Lyle's coffin."

Perry yanked on his line and reeled in another trout, which he added to the string. When it came to hunting and fishing, he was second to none. His skill kept them well-supplied with trout and venison. And he was, as Raymond had mentioned, highly intelligent.

The problem Boone had with Perry was that he tended to go his own way. When he thought he was right, he broke ranks. Innately dangerous and coldly sadistic, Perry was the ultimate weapon, but Boone had to be sure he was aimed in the right direction.

"Another thing," Perry said to Raymond. "I'm not smarter than Boone. He's our leader. And don't you ever forget it."

Boone smiled as he slipped his gun back into his pocket. Perry still believed in him and trusted his authority. Good!

When Boone stepped out from the trees, both Perry and Raymond reached for their rifles. Perry's beady black eyes narrowed. "Shouldn't sneak up on a man like that. It's a good way to get your head blown off."

"I trust your reflexes," Boone said. "Even in the dark, you'd know it was me."

Though there was still a slight question in his mind about whether Perry might shoot him even if he did recognize him, Boone didn't show his lack of confidence.

"Were you spying on us?" Perry asked.

"I was looking for you. We need to talk." Boone faced him directly. "By the way, I know that you went to Lyle's funeral. I'm glad. Lyle was a good man."

"The best," Perry said. "What's up?"

He stood between the two men. "I have a plan."

"I sure as hell hope it turns out better than the last two plans," Perry muttered. He reached inside his jacket and pulled an eight inch long serrated knife from a sheath on his belt. "I don't want any more funerals."

"Yeah," Raymond chimed in. "And I'm sick of doing the dirty work for that bastard, the Puppetmaster. Who does he think he is? We're free men. We're nobody's puppets."

"That's true," Boone said. But the so-called Puppetmaster had been responsible for their escape from the Fortress. His demands were not to be taken lightly. "This time he wants the same thing we do."

"What's that?" Perry separated one of the writhing trout from the line. The fish was a decent size— twelve inches long. With a neat flick of his blade, Perry sliced open the belly and tore out the guts.

"Remember five years ago." Boone spoke in a whisper, compelling the other men to lean toward him. "Remember when we blew up the federal building?"

"Hell, yes." Perry rinsed the fish in the icy stream and reattached it to a line. "We made a statement."

"We're going to do it again."

"Another bomb?" The sunrise reflected on Perry's weathered, pockmarked face. "Where?"

"A public place." Boone spread the full glory of his plan before them as though he was offering a golden treasure. "We take hostages and lay siege. Then we wait. Patiently. And allow the media to do their work."

"I don't get it," Raymond said. "If we do that, every cop in Montana will be there."

"Every cop," Perry repeated. "And the feds. And the National Guard."

Boone nodded. "And the unknown pursuers who keep coming after us—the men who messed up our last two missions. They won't be able to stay away. Not while we're holding innocent lives in our hands."

A smile broke across Perry's face. "They'll have to show themselves."

"Once we know who they are," Boone said, "we can take them out."

He paused, allowing the full cleverness of his plan to sink in. Not only would he satisfy the demands of the Puppetmaster and flush out their unknown nemesis, but the Militia would also have their just revenge. "Sierra Collins will be the first hostage to die."

AT THE BIG SKY GALLERIA mall in Helena, Sierra stood behind the counter of Olson's Outdoor Sporting Goods. Over her jeans and blue work shirt, she wore a Day-Glo-orange hunting vest—the standard uniform for the clerks at the store—and she chatted knowledgeably with a customer about the merits of fly rods and spinner reels.

If her friends back in Brooklyn could see her now, they'd never believe it. Not that Sierra had ever been a girlie girl. When it came to playing stickball or hoops, she kicked butt. But she was never interested in camping. Hunting and fishing? Forget about it.

She rang up the customer's purchase and checked her wristwatch. It was half past five. Her shift today ended at six. Three days a week, she spent over an hour on the road, driving to Helena for this clerk job. Next month, when the winter snows hit and the roads got bad, it wouldn't be worth her time to make the difficult journey unless she could convince her supervisor at Olson's Outdoor Sporting Goods to hire her full-time. Then she'd move here to Helena.

The telephone on the desk beside the register rang, and she picked up. "Olson's Outdoor Sporting Goods. How may I help you?"

"Sierra Collins."

"Who's this?"

"Someone who used to be a friend."

Startled, she recognized the rasping voice. And she remembered his scarred face, his scraggly beard, his cruel dark eyes. "Boone Fowler."

"Very good. You were always smart for a girl."

Her gaze darted wildly around the store. Boone Fowler was a fugitive. She ought to tell someone about this call, ought to notify the authorities. The only other clerk in the store was busy with a customer who was buying a hunting rifle.

If Sierra called out for help and mentioned the Militia, she'd probably be gunned down where she stood. "What do you want, Boone?"

"What do you think?"

"I think you expect an apology," she said. "Because I spat on the grave of your best friend, Lyle."

"Your fiancé," he said.

"Don't remind me. Lyle was the worst mistake I ever made. He can burn in hell."

"But he owed you. Didn't he?"

"Damn right, he did."

"I want to correct that situation." He was slick as a snake oil salesman. "I understand the wrong that's been done to you, and I want to make sure you get everything that's coming to you."

She didn't trust Boone Fowler. He was vicious and cruel. Under his influence, Lyle had become a mean son of a bitch. "I don't believe you."

"Lyle had a considerable amount of money. I'll

give you a share. All I ask in return is that you keep your mouth shut."

Her clenched fist pounded lightly on the glass countertop. Why did everybody think she knew something important? Trevor thought she had information. Now Boone.

"Sierra, you want the money. You need it." He knew just the right thing to say—the promise that would hook her attention. "I'll meet you in a public place. The Galleria where you work. Today is Monday. How about Wednesday?"

"I don't work on Wednesday. Only Thursday and Friday this week."

"Fine," he said. "I'll see you then."

The phone went dead in her hand. When she replaced the receiver on the hook, her fingers were trembling. Why had she told him her work schedule? Nothing good could come from further contact with the Militia.

Sierra stepped out from behind the counter and busied herself with refolding T-shirts. Her mind raced. Should she say something about the call? Alert the police? Half the law enforcement personnel in Montana were looking for the Militia. But if she admitted that Boone had contacted her, Sierra feared she would come under suspicion.

On the other hand, if she told the police that the fugitive Boone Fowler was coming to the mall and he found out, Boone would surely kill her.

It was better not to speak. Not right now, anyway. She had until Thursday to think about it.

She clocked out at six and went to her car in the parking lot. Though she was driving east, away from the sunset, a reflected amber brilliance spanned the wide-open skies and colored the autumn leaves at the forested edge of the foothills.

For a moment, as she drove, she forgot about her lack of money, her lousy jobs and this new threat from Boone Fowler. The stunning beauty of Montana was too much to ignore. She remembered back when she'd been first dating Lyle, and he'd talked about the land that he loved. He had seduced her with Montana, showing her a velvet night sky filled with more stars than she could ever count. He'd given her rushing rivers, majestic peaks and sun-filled days. He'd warned her that nature could be cruel. Then he'd shown her the meaning of pain.

When Lyle died, that part of her life—the part that was associated with the Militia—should have been over. Why had Boone called her? What if he actually did have money for her? Lyle had stolen her nest egg, close to four thousand dollars. If she had that money back, it would make a world of difference.

But why would Boone Fowler do her any favors? He was more likely to slit her throat than to say hello.

When she parked on the street outside her duplex, Trevor's black Jeep was waiting for her.

"Swell," she muttered. Here was another man who only wanted to manipulate her.

In his flat-brimmed hat and shearling jacket, Trevor was far more handsome than any of the men she'd met in the Militia, including Lyle. But good looks were no excuse for what he'd done to her. He'd forcibly carried her off on horseback and imprisoned her. She still couldn't remember what had happened in that little room, but her instincts told her it wasn't good.

He leaned down to her window and spoke through the glass. "I brought you a present."

She shoved the car door into him and got out. "I don't want anything from you."

"Why not?"

"Because there are always strings attached." And that was the real problem with Boone's offer of money. Yes, she deserved it. Yes, she wanted it. But she hated to imagine what Boone would ask in return. "Leave me alone, Trevor."

"Come on," he urged. "Before you say no, take a look."

"I don't want anything to do with you. Or your friends." Angrily she added, "By the way, the guy who brought my car back to my house left the seat pushed way back."

"It's not my fault that he's taller than you. And I told you we needed to check your car for damage before we returned it."

"There's no reason my Nissan would be damaged."

"You ticked off those Militia wannabes at the funeral. They could come after you."

"But they didn't."

When she turned on her heel and started toward her front door, he caught hold of her arm. "Wait."

"Let go of me."

Immediately he loosened his grasp. But he didn't back off. "Aren't you curious about what I got for you? I thought about it a long time. It's the perfect gift."

"You don't know me. You have no idea about what's perfect for me."

"I know you're practical. You're not a flowers-and-candy kind of woman."

"So?"

"This gift is practical."

At the rear of his Jeep he pulled open the door, revealing several white boxes. The words *Finest Angus* were printed on the side.

"Beef," he said proudly. "I got you a side of beef."

His gift couldn't have been more wrong or less practical. "I'm a vegetarian."

"A what?"

"If it has a face, I don't eat it."

He yanked his hat off his head and looked up as if imploring the moon. "What kind of person lives in cattle country and doesn't eat beef?"

"A vegetarian."

She slammed the back door of his Jeep with a satisfying thud and marched up the sidewalk. As she approached the concrete stoop leading to the door on her side of the clapboard duplex, the gray-haired woman who lived next door emerged. Sierra gave her a friendly wave. "Good evening, Mrs. Hensley."

As usual, Mrs. Hensley stuck her nose in the air, proceeded down the sidewalk and turned right, heading toward Main Street.

Trevor stepped onto the porch behind her. "How come she snubbed you?"

"Are you still here?"

"I intend to escort you inside and make sure your house is safe." His tone was deadly serious. "You might not think you're in danger, but I do."

Sierra remembered the day—not that long ago—when Lyle had broken in to her house and waited for her. A shudder went through her. That scene was something she never wanted to happen again. "Okay. You come inside and look around. Then you leave. Understood?"

"Whatever you want."

He took the key from her hand, unlocked the front door and slowly pushed it open. "So what's the deal with your neighbor?"

"I like to tell myself that her hearing aid isn't working, but it's more likely that Mrs. Hensley doesn't approve of me. She hates the Militia."

"So do you."

"Doesn't matter."

She followed him inside and turned on the overhead light in the small front room. If she'd been back in Brooklyn, she would have called her décor "shabby chic." Out here, there was no need for pretense. It was plain old shabby.

In minutes, Trevor had searched the whole house. He returned to her side. "I'd feel a lot better if you had someone stay with you."

"I don't need a babysitter."

"Maybe a friend," he suggested.

"I don't have many friends in Ponderosa. The ones who are sympathetic to the Militia abandoned me when I dumped Lyle. And those who despise the Militia don't want anything to do with me. That's why I had to go all the way to Helena to find a job."

"But you have another job here."

"At the tree nursery. The old guy who runs it is one of those rugged individuals who doesn't care what anybody else thinks. But he can only give me two days a week. Tuesday and Wednesday."

"Do you like working outside?"

"Why am I talking to you?" She stalked through the front room to the kitchen, opened the refrigerator and took out a bottled beer. Over her shoulder she said, "You promised to leave."

"Just for the record," he said, "tell me what vegetarians like to eat."

"Vegetables." She screwed off the top of the beer

and took a sip. "And don't bother showing up on my doorstep with a truckload of produce. I won't accept gifts from you, Trevor. I don't like you."

Her outright antagonism didn't faze him in the least. He stood in her doorway as though he had every right to be there. Grudgingly she had to admire his determination. He didn't give up easily.

"What's your favorite food?" he asked.

"Cannolis," she muttered

"What?"

"Cannolis from this great little bakery in Brooklyn. Pure heaven." Just thinking about those creamy sugary pastries made her mouth water. "You've probably never even heard of cannolis."

"I'll eat just about anything, except potatoes. I grew up on a potato farm in Idaho."

As soon as he spoke, she knew she'd heard those words before. When he was questioning her? She'd been in that little room for four hours. They must have talked for a long time, but their conversation was mostly a blank. It wasn't right that he'd stolen those hours from her life. She wanted to know what had been said.

Another detail came clear in her mind. "You're part Cherokee."

"On my father's side."

"Your Cherokee father was a potato farmer?"

"The farm belonged to my mother's family. I never knew my dad. It wasn't until I was an adult that

I got interested in my Native American background."
He held out his hand and showed her a silver ring
with a seven-pointed star. "This is the symbol of the
Cherokee nation."

In spite of herself, she was interested. "You're
proud of your heritage."

He gave a quick nod. "But I spent the first half of
my life denying it. I was a half-breed. Didn't fit in
with either side."

It was hard for her to believe. "A big, handsome
guy like you shouldn't have any problem making
friends."

"I could say the same about you, Sierra. From
what you've said, nobody in Ponderosa likes you.
And you're beautiful."

Surprised by his compliment, she met his gaze.
His clear blue eyes were sincere; he wasn't joking.
There was a tenderness in his manner that reached
out and touched her.

Quickly she looked away. This was the same man
who'd tied her up and asked hard questions—questions she couldn't quite remember. He'd kidnapped
her. He was capable of cruelty. The dumbest thing
she could possibly do was to fall for another man
from Montana.

"Are you trying to snow me, Trevor?"

"I speak only the truth."

"How totally Cherokee of you."

"I am what I am."

"One of the good guys?" She sipped her beer. "I don't generally think of bounty hunters as clean-cut, upstanding members of the community."

"We have our moments," he said. "That's the biggest reason I'm here. I have concerns about your safety. You insulted the Militia, and they're not known for being forgiving."

"I'm fine," she said quickly.

"I could stay with you," he said. "Protect you."

"Stay with me? As in, stay at my house?" She vigorously shook her head. "That's not going to happen."

"Sierra, I didn't mean—"

"I know what you're after." He thought she was an easy mark. Because she'd been crazy enough to fall in love with Lyle, Trevor thought she was the kind of woman who tumbled into the sack with every mangy cowboy who crossed her path.

"I'm after the Militia." The tenderness vanished from his face. When he talked about the Militia, his features hardened. "They might want to teach you a lesson."

She rolled her eyes. "So, you're not interested in sleeping with me?"

He raised the beer bottle to his mouth and took a drink. Clearly, he was avoiding her question.

"Come on, Trevor. You just said you never lie."

"Truth?"

"Yeah."

"You're right, Sierra. I want to make love to you. That's the only thing I've been thinking about since I saw you standing beside Lyle Nelson's grave."

In spite of her hostility, an undeniable thrill raced up and down her spine. He'd been thinking about her? Constantly? "Maybe that was a little too much honesty."

"Get ready for more," he said.

"There's more?"

"I also want to catch the Militia."

Catching the Militia? How was that related to making love? "So, you want to be with me because you think Boone Fowler and his merry band of jerks might come after me?"

Trevor gave a quick nod. "Right."

"I get it," she said. "You want to use me as bait."

"If I had a choice, I'd hide you away where you'd be safe. I'd give you enough money to get back to your family in Brooklyn." He shook his head. "But you won't let that happen. You're too stubborn. Too proud."

She wasn't sure which of his statements was the most infuriating. That he thought she'd invite him into her bed? That she was too stubborn? That he wanted to dangle her like a worm on a hook in front of the Militia?

Thank God she hadn't told him about the call from Boone Fowler. She wouldn't trust Trevor with her grocery list.

She raised her arm and pointed toward the door. "Get out of my life. Now."

Chapter Five

Driving hard and fast on the narrow roads leading to Big Sky Bounty Hunters headquarters, Trevor listened to the surveillance bug he'd planted in Sierra's duplex. The sound of her television mingled with common household noises. There was the scrape of a chair leg against the worn wood floor in her kitchen, the rush of water in the sink, the clank of a pot being placed on the stovetop.

Apparently, she was preparing dinner. Some kind of nonmeat food. Pasta or rice or something. "Vegetarian," he muttered.

When he'd had her in the interrogation room and under the influence of the TD, he should have asked about her eating habits. Instead, he'd gone out and bought a mountain of red meat that he presented to her with the chest-thumping pride of a caveman who had just clubbed his first brontosaurus. Idiot! Trevor had never been good with women, but this meeting with Sierra ranked among the worst.

His headlights slashed through the night, illuminating the thick conifers, as he whipped into a sharp right turn.

Over the bug, he heard a tuneless humming from Sierra. Too easily, he visualized her lush, beautiful body. In his mind's eye, he saw her reaching up to a high shelf with her arm arched and her wrist turned gracefully.

He heard her chuckle softly and remembered the adorable way her nose crinkled when she laughed. Damn! The woman had rejected him, and he still couldn't stop thinking about her, imagining her every move. Did he want to spend the night in her bed? Hell, yes.

He turned off the sound on the listening device. Later, he'd return to her duplex for an all-night stakeout. Right now, he needed to put some distance between himself and Sierra Collins.

He parked at headquarters, went around to the back of his Jeep and grabbed two boxes of fine Angus steaks, which he carried up the stairs to the pantry behind the kitchen. He yanked open the freezer and stored the beef inside.

"Blackhaw?" Tony Lombardi poked his head into the pantry. "What's up?"

"I was in Helena today and bought a side of beef. Help me get the rest of it."

Lombardi followed him outside. "What were you doing in Helena?"

"Surveillance on Sierra Collins. She works there. At the Galleria mall."

Between them, they hauled the rest of the beef inside. Trevor couldn't close the door to the freezer fast enough. It was embarrassing to look at those boxes he'd thought would make a perfect gift for Sierra. "You're from New York, Lombardi. Tell me about cannolis."

"Italian pastry. A flaky shell wrapped around creamy, sugary frosting." He licked his lips. "So sweet it makes your teeth ache."

"Is there anyplace around here where I can get one?"

Lombardi scoffed. "Not a chance. Nobody makes cannolis like you get in the Bronx or Brooklyn."

Together, they went into the large front room, where Riley Watson sprawled in front of the fireplace, reading a newspaper. Watson's usually dark hair was dyed blond and he looked younger than his thirty-six years.

Trevor wasn't surprised by the unusual appearance. Watson was a master of disguise who switched identities quicker than most men changed shirts.

"Hey, Blackhaw," Watson drawled.

Trevor nodded. "Anything new?"

Watson glanced at the headlines. "Prince Nikolai of Lukinburg made a big speech about terrorism. Ever since the Petrov royal family showed up in Montana, the local news can't get enough of them."

Trevor couldn't care less about politics, local or international. "Anything new on the Militia?"

"I spent most of the day shoveling a lot of dirt to see if I could uncover a lead. I talked to people all over Ponderosa."

"I bet," Lombardi said. "And you charmed the pants off the females. All the chicks love that Texas drawl."

"There's this cute little checker at the supermarket." Watson grinned. "She told me that some guy came in this afternoon and bought twelve gallons of ammonia. From her description, it could have been Raymond Fleming."

Though the information didn't seem to be particularly useful, Trevor was eager to hear more. Their leads had been few and far between. "Why ammonia?"

"I don't think it's because the Militia is planning to start a housecleaning service," Watson drawled. "Ammonia can be used in bomb making."

Another bomb. Definitely bad news. "We need to check the purchase of other components."

"Already being done. We're going through computer records in case they're dumb enough to use a credit card. Tomorrow, we'll stake out hardware stores and hobby shops." Watson rose from his chair, stretched and yawned. "How about you, Blackhaw? What are you up to?"

Lombardi provided the answer. "He's been keeping an eye on Lyle Nelson's girlfriend."

"Is Sierra Collins as pretty as her photo?" Watson asked.

Trevor made a quick pivot and headed toward the door. "I'm going out to the barn to—"

"Whoa, there," Watson said. "I'm sensing something here. Blackhaw, have you got a thing for Miss Sierra Collins?"

Lombardi pounced. "That's why you were asking me about cannolis. She's from Brooklyn. I bet she wants a cannoli. Am I right?"

Trevor continued toward the back door. "I'm going to check on the horses."

Though he hadn't invited Watson or Lombardi along, they were on his heels as he unlatched the door to the well-maintained barn, where half a dozen horses were kept. Trevor went first to the stall occupied by his favorite mustang stallion, Smokey.

The horse nickered a greeting, and Trevor reached up to scratch behind his ears. "Hey, boy."

"Hey yourself," Watson said. "What's going on with you and Sierra?"

Though Trevor would have preferred to spend his time tending to the horses—a chore he always found relaxing—there was nothing to do. The barn had already been mucked out and the horses neatly bedded down for the night.

He turned to face his two co-workers. He'd worked with these guys for years, and they knew him too well for him to keep a secret. Trevor shrugged. "Maybe I see something special in Sierra."

Watson leaned his lanky frame against the wood

slats of a stall. "You're going to have to give us more than that."

"I wouldn't expect you two to understand. You're both slick when it comes to getting a date."

"You do okay." Lombardi bent down to pick up a piece of straw, which he twisted around his forefinger. "I know what happens when I walk into a bar with you. All those pretty little women turn around and stare. At you, Blackhaw. You're a chick magnet."

"True," Watson said. "You can score anytime."

"This is different," Trevor said.

With other women, he was aware of holding back, never sharing the deeper part of himself. With Sierra, he had an unexplainable urge to tell her everything about his life. His pain. His frustrations. His moments of greatest joy and deepest sorrow. "I can't explain it."

"Give it a try," Watson urged. "Not that I'm interrogating you or anything."

Trevor shot him a cold glare. "Don't go there. I never use interrogation techniques in everyday life, and you don't want me to start."

Watson wasn't the least bit intimidated. "What happened between you and Sierra?"

"I wanted to get her something nice. You know, a gift. But she's a practical woman and…"

"What?"

"I got her a side of beef."

Watson exchanged a glance with Lombardi . "Not a real romantic gift."

"Seemed like the right thing to do." During the time he'd spent at the Cherokee nation, he'd learned that a gift of meat was a special honor, symbolic of commitment. That thought might have subconsciously influenced his choice.

"But she didn't like the beef," Watson said.

"She's a vegetarian."

Lombardi groaned. "Talk about a giant screwup."

"Then," Trevor said, "she asked me point-blank if I was trying to get her into bed."

"Let me guess," Watson said. "You said yes."

"I was being honest."

"Bad idea," Lombardi said. "But here's how you can make it up to her. I've got an address in the Bronx where you can order air express cannolis."

It was worth a try, but Trevor expected that it would take more than Italian pastry to impress a woman who pretty much hated his guts.

ON WEDNESDAY MORNING, Trevor's second day of full-time surveillance on Sierra, he sat by the window in a diner on Spruce Street. Sipping his third mug of thick black coffee, he stared across the road at the office of Ponderosa Tree Nursery, where Sierra worked two days a week. In her tight little jeans, she bounced down the three stairs from the office and headed toward the enclosed greenhouse. She'd started the day wearing an overlarge flannel shirt, but had now stripped down to a navy-blue tee. Her thick, honey-blond curls were pulled up in a ponytail that stuck out the back of a New York Yankees baseball cap.

She was damn cute, but Trevor couldn't help wondering if watching her was a waste of time. After scouting the perimeter of the twenty-acre nursery, and lurking around on side streets and coming to this homely little diner for every meal, he had observed nothing that made him think the Militia was interested in her.

The only tangible result of his constant observation of Sierra Collins was Trevor turning into a drooling lunatic. He wasn't the type of man who liked to watch, and it was driving him crazy not to touch her. From afar, he had memorized her shape as she did physical labor—bending, digging, transplanting and unloading trucks. She was strong, but with that perfect hourglass figure, she was not in the least bit masculine. Her delectable curves, he decided, were second to none.

With a morose sigh, he looked up from his coffee as Cameron Murphy entered the diner and slid into the booth opposite him. He placed an air express package on the tabletop. "How's it going, Blackhaw?"

"It's pretty damn slow, sir."

His former commanding officer gave him a sympathetic grin, and Trevor wondered if Lombardi and Watson had blabbed about his attraction to Sierra. Trevor hoped not. He didn't want to be pegged among the bounty hunters as a lovesick fool.

"You need to continue surveillance on the tree nursery," Murphy said as he signaled the waitress for coffee. "You're doing more than keeping an eye on Sierra."

In an instant, Trevor went from gloomy lethargy to full alert. Something was up. Murphy had taken the trouble of coming here physically rather than contacting him on the cell phone.

"As you know," Murphy continued, "we suspect the Militia are assembling the components for a bomb. There was an unusually large purchase of ethyl alcohol from a hardware store. Yesterday, a hobby shop in Helena sold the material necessary to make fuses."

Murphy paused as the waitress placed his coffee mug on the table. She snapped her gum. "Cream?" she asked.

"Thank you, no." Murphy smiled up at her.

She turned and winked at Trevor. "How about you, honey? Want a blueberry muffin? It's on the house."

He'd been spending so much time here that he'd developed a relationship with the waitress. He knew that she dyed her hair blond to cover the gray and that her gum-chewing was supposed to help her quit smoking. "Not right now, Ginny."

"If you boys want anything at all, give me a shout."

"You bet," Trevor said. He leaned toward Murphy. "Go on."

"This morning," he stated, "we learned about the theft of potassium cyanide from a metal processing and welding shop. That substance is used in the electroplating process."

"What else is it used for?"

"Potassium cyanide is a lethal nerve agent."

Tension shot through Trevor's body. "What happens when someone is exposed to it?"

"It's nasty stuff. If breathed in or passed through the skin, there's an immediate irritation, especially to the eyes. Possible blindness. Then nosebleed and a pounding headache. The final result is irreparable damage to the central nervous system, thyroid enlargement, possible heart attack. And death."

"And you believe the Militia has this substance?"

"I do." Murphy raised his coffee mug to his lips. "And I believe they'll use it."

The churning in Trevor's gut had nothing to do with the amount of caffeine he'd consumed in the past hour. It seemed that the Militia was on the verge of returning to their former terrorist ways."

"We'll stop them," Trevor said.

"I want to believe that." Murphy reached up and rubbed his bum shoulder, which Trevor knew had been injured in a confrontation with Boone Fowler. "I thought when the Militia were locked up in the Fortress with no chance for parole, this battle was won."

No battle was truly ended until the enemy was dead.

Even then, according to Cherokee belief, the ghost of a lifelong adversary might return. "Have you notified law enforcement about the bomb components?"

"State, local and federal," Murphy said. "They've placed extra guards in all government buildings."

But he sounded doubtful. At the edge of his strength and determination, Trevor sensed a wavering apprehension. It wasn't fear. Cameron Murphy wasn't afraid of anything, but much had changed for him in five years. He was married now and had a child.

"The security at government buildings is better now than it used to be," Trevor said. "Everything tightened up after 9-11. The Militia won't get through."

"They could strike anywhere. On a bus in Helena. During a high school football game. At a preschool."

Murphy's voice faded. His gaze turned inward, and Trevor knew he was thinking of his beautiful four-year-old daughter, Olivia.

"Sir," Trevor said, "we won't let that happen. What do you want me to do?"

"Continue surveillance on the tree nursery. Other components for bomb making are sulfur and sodium nitrate. Both are used in fertilizers."

"Fertilizer," Trevor grumbled. "You want me to stay here and keep an eye on the mulch?"

"And Sierra," he said. "I know you think she's innocent as a newborn lamb, but she does have access to the chemicals needed by the Militia. She might still be working with them."

"No, sir. She hates the Militia."

"How can you be sure?"

"I interrogated her." Inwardly, Trevor winced at the painful memory. "I broke her down. She's not involved with the Militia. Not in any way."

Murphy finished off his coffee and rose from the booth. He tapped the air express package he'd placed on the table when he first arrived. "Lombardi said you should open this right away."

As Murphy sauntered toward the exit, Trevor noticed Ginny studying him with admiring eyes. She bustled over to the table to freshen Trevor's coffee. "Your friend," she said, "is he married?"

"Very much so."

"Doggone it! All the good ones are taken."

"I'm hurt." Trevor clutched his chest. "I'm not married."

"You might as well be. Trevor, honey, you can't take your eyes off that cute gal who works at the tree nursery. Don't think I haven't noticed you staring at her and sighing like a lovesick calf."

He scoffed. "I don't sigh."

"Fooled me." She stepped back from the table and nodded toward the window. "And it looks like you're in luck, because she's on her way over here right now."

He hadn't been watching. While he'd been preoccupied, Sierra had crossed the road from the nursery. She was at the door to the diner.

Fine. It was time they came face-to-face. For a day

and a half, he'd respected her wish to have him out of her life. He hadn't approached her or spoken to her. But his surveillance on her home and workplace hadn't been a covert operation. If she'd been even halfway alert, she would have noticed his Jeep.

She strolled into the diner. Her pace was casual, but her dark-eyed gaze flicked from table to counter to booth until she was looking directly at him. With her lush hips swinging, she came toward him and slid into the booth, filling the space that had been occupied moments ago by Cameron Murphy.

"Trevor," she said.

"Sierra."

A long moment of silence stretched between them, He noticed a smudge of fresh dirt on her chin. In spite of the brimmed Yankees' cap, she had a touch of sunburn on her cheeks. "You've been following me," she said.

"I told you before—I'm concerned about your safety."

Ginny came to the table. "What can I get you?"

"A strawberry milkshake with whipped cream on top."

"Coming right up."

Sierra turned her attention to Trevor again. "Don't expect a thank-you for protecting me. As I'm sure you realize by now, it wasn't necessary."

"It's still possible that the Militia will contact you."

When she glanced down at the beige Formica tabletop, he caught a glimpse of an attitude that worried him. Though Trevor wasn't trained in reading body language like Mike Clark, he recognized the signals. Her lips pinched together, holding back the truth. Sierra was behaving like a person who had something to hide.

Trevor remembered Murphy's suspicion that she might still be in contact with the Militia. They might use her to get their hands on the chemicals needed for bomb-making. "Sierra, is there something you want to tell me?"

"I have a feeling that I already told you too much." She rested her fingertips on the table and stared down at them. "It's a funny thing. Not funny as in ha-ha, but weird funny. When I woke up in that horrible little room, I couldn't remember what we talked about."

He said nothing. Though he had promised to tell her the truth, now wasn't the time for him to confess that he'd used a truth drug and then a hypnotic suggestion to relieve her painful memories.

"I keep getting flashes," she said. "I remember a darkness. A disconnected static noise. Then I hear my own voice talking." Her fingers tapped a nervous tattoo on the table. "Why can't I remember?"

"Sometimes it's better not to question."

"Wrong." She looked up at him. "If there's one thing I learned from being engaged to Lyle, it was that I need to know the truth."

"Know this." Trevor reached across the table and

covered her hands with his. "You said nothing in-criminating. Nothing that made me think less of you."

"As if your opinion matters to me?"

She lifted her chin. Her fixed gaze challenged him, but beyond her apparent hostility was a raging heat. He felt her drawing closer to him. Whether she liked it or not, the magnetic pull between them was an irresistible force.

Did she remember their kiss in the interrogation room? He sure as hell remembered that moment when he'd held her pliant body in his arms. She'd called to him. She'd asked him to kiss her, and he'd responded. The taste of her warm honeyed lips was indelibly imprinted in his sensory memory.

Abruptly, she leaned back in the booth and pointed to the air express package. "What's this?"

"Let's take a look."

Using his pocketknife, he cut the tape on the pack-age, which had a return address in the Bronx. Ac-cording to Murphy, Lombardi wanted him to open it right away. Trevor peeled off the paper and revealed a white cardboard box. The stamp on the top said Angelo's Bakery.

Trevor lifted the lid. Inside were six pastries. He turned the box toward Sierra. "For you."

"Cannolis. Oh my God!"

Finally, he'd done something she approved of.

With satisfaction, he leaned back in the booth and watched as she savored the first bite of cannoli. A lusty moan escaped her lips. She gasped. Then moaned again.

"Hey, now." Ginny returned to their booth with the strawberry milkshake. "What's going on over here?"

"Cannoli." Sierra licked powdered sugar from her mouth and glanced up at the waitress. "I'm telling you, this is better than sex."

She grabbed Trevor's pocketknife and cut off a piece for Ginny. "Try it."

The waitress tasted the pastry. "Oh, yes."

"From New York," Sierra said. "Trevor got them for me."

Ginny gave him a grin. "I guess you know the way to a woman's heart."

"Through her cannolis," Sierra said.

She cut off another piece and passed it to Trevor. He took a bite. The sugary, creamy texture melted on his tongue. "Good."

"That's it? Good?" Sierra stared at him. "It's great. Totally."

The sugar rush lowered her defenses, and she chatted happily as she worked her way through the milkshake and another cannoli. For the first time, there seemed to be no hidden agenda between them, no secrets.

He found himself beginning to hope that she might trust him. He pressed the advantage. "You know, Sierra, since I'm going to keep watching you anyway, we might as well spend this time together."

"Give it up," she said. "Nobody's after me. You don't have to keep watching me."

"You're still my best lead."

She glanced up at him, then quickly lowered her gaze to the sugar feast spread before her on the Formica table. Her guard went up again.

He asked, "Have you been contacted?"

She scooted to the edge of the booth. Before she could stand, he caught hold of her forearm. His grasp was firm. "Sierra, these men are dangerous."

"You don't have to tell me that."

"You're not the only one in peril." How much could he tell her about the bomb-making? If she was in contact with Boone Fowler, she might pass the information along. "If you know anything about their whereabouts, you've got to tell me."

"I don't know where they are." She pulled her arm from his grasp and closed the lid on the cannoli box. Standing, she dug three bucks from her back pocket and placed them on the table. "This is for the milk-shake. Thanks for the cannolis. Way better than beef."

Before he could ask another question, she darted toward the exit of the diner. The door slammed shut behind her.

Through the window, he watched her cross the road and return to her job at the nursery. Damn it! He knew she was keeping something from him, something about the Militia.

When she was under the influence of the truth

drug, she'd said that she hated them. And Trevor believed her. He'd swear that she was not sympathetic to Boone Fowler, but she didn't understand the urgency or the danger to herself. And others.

Chapter Six

The next morning, Sierra left her duplex at a few minutes before eight so she'd have time to get to her job at the Galleria by nine-thirty. She hadn't slept well. Her dreams were haunted by visions of Boone Fowler and Perry Johnson, his sadistic sidekick. On the phone, Boone had said he'd see her today or tomorrow at the Galleria. He'd said she'd get what she deserved, and she really didn't think he was talking about her share of the loot.

She closed her front door gently so she wouldn't disturb her neighbor. The October morning was chilly, and her breath frosted the air. In her front yard, the autumn leaves clung stubbornly to the shivering branches of the cottonwood tree.

As she strode down the sidewalk, she glared at Trevor's Jeep, which was parked directly behind her car on the street. He emerged from the driver's side, leaned across the hood and nodded to her, making no effort to hide the fact that he was keeping surveillance.

She called out, "Give it up, Trevor."

"Good morning, Sierra."

"I mean it," she said. "You don't have to watch me."

"We'll see."

The man was relentless.

Without saying another word to him, she slid behind the wheel of her little Nissan. A glance in the rearview mirror showed that he was back in his car—ready to follow her to work.

In some ways, it was reassuring to have a big, tall, handsome bounty hunter as a full-time bodyguard. Kind of like a guardian angel. She scoffed. Trevor? Angelic? When she thought of him, saintliness was the last thing that came to mind.

Her reliable little car started up on the first try, and she pulled away from the curb. She kept to the speed limit in Ponderosa, where the local sheriff liked to hand out tickets, but when she merged onto the two-lane route leading to Helena, Sierra hit the gas. There wasn't much traffic, wasn't much of anything except an incredible panorama of buttes, promontories and distant, snow-capped peaks. This had to be the most scenic commute in the world, especially for Sierra, who had grown up riding the subway.

When she came to Montana, she hadn't known what to expect. In the back of her mind, she might have been thinking she'd find herself a man who was nearly as spectacular as the landscape. A handsome cowboy with tight jeans and broad shoulders—a man like Trevor.

Last night, when she'd looked out her front window before going to bed, she'd seen him leaning against the pole of the corner streetlight. In his shearling coat, with his arms folded across his chest, and his flat-brim hat, he was the very archetype of a cowboy. Strong and silent. A manly man.

She sighed. Last night, she could have invited him into her home, could have offered to share the cannolis, could have had some friendly conversation. Yeah, right! As if they'd spend the night talking! She was pretty darn sure what would happen if she opened the door to Trevor. He'd been truthful about wanting to get her into the sack. If she lowered her guard, there would be touching and kissing and everything that came after that.

Was that such a bad thing?

Damn right, it was! She'd already allowed herself to be swept away by her cowboy fantasies with Lyle. Look how badly that turned out! There would be no more cowboys in her life. Not now. Not ever.

She turned on her car radio. The local newscaster was babbling about Prince Nikolai Petrov of Lukinburg. Ever since his visit to Helena, the people of Montana were fascinated with him. Not that Sierra blamed anybody for their interest. Nikolai was a real live prince—like in the fairy tales. And judging from his photos in the newspaper and on television, he was gorgeous with thick, curly black hair and sexy bedroom eyes. Not to mention the tailored Armani suits.

As a bonus, Nikolai had principles. He'd stood up to his dictator father and denounced the terrorism in his country, which was exactly what he was doing this morning in an address to the United Nations. His accented baritone came over the radio. "Terrorism is an international disease, and my homeland, Lukinburg, is infected. The United Nations must intervene. The terrorists are everywhere. They could strike anywhere. And they must be stopped."

Sierra replied to the radio. "Damn right, Prince."

As a native New Yorker, she was no stranger to terrorism. Her grip on the steering wheel tightened. She'd lost two friends on 9-11. When she thought of that terrible day, she felt anger—a boundless rage against cowards who attacked innocent people.

Terrorists were everywhere. Even in Montana.

She glanced in her rearview mirror and spotted Trevor's Jeep. Should she tell him about the phone call from Boone Fowler? Trevor already suspected her of being in contact with the Militia. If she confirmed his suspicion, he'd be obliged to tell the police. Then she'd be taken into custody for questioning—an ordeal she never wanted to live through again. After Lyle and the other Militia were arrested, she'd been grilled like a trout, answered a thousand questions by law enforcement officers with suspicious eyes. Interrogators. Like Trevor.

Those were the darkest days of her whole life. She'd been so isolated. Then she lost the baby. Her son.

"Damn you, Lyle. You got what you deserved."

She turned the radio to an all-music station and cranked up the volume, hoping to drown out the dialogue inside her head. More than likely, Boone had told her he was coming because he wanted to scare her. He wouldn't show.

But if he did?

She glanced in her rearview mirror again. Her decision was made. She would tell Trevor about that phone call.

HANGING OUT IN A MALL HAD never been Trevor's idea of a good time. On Monday, when he followed Sierra, he had already discovered just about everything he wanted to know about the Big Sky Galleria in Helena. There was a food court and two big department stores, one on each end. The mall itself was two stories tall, open to the ceiling, with shops lining the walkways on both levels. Standing at a railing on the second floor, he looked down into the first-floor sporting goods store where Sierra worked.

His position provided a good surveillance point, even though he didn't need to worry about having Sierra notice his presence. She damn well knew he was following her.

Last night, when she'd peeked out her front window and seen him, Trevor thought she might invite him inside. She'd stared for a long time before she let the curtain close, and turned out the lights. Apparently, she didn't care that he was bored to death and freezing his butt off.

After sleeping in his Jeep night after night, he was on edge, anxious for something to happen. And he wasn't the only one. From cell phone contact with the rest of the bounty hunters, Trevor knew they all shared his mood. Watching and waiting, they were on high alert, aware that a bomb attack from the Militia might be imminent.

He strolled over to the escalator and went downstairs, figuring he might convince Sierra to join him for coffee on her morning break.

The store right next to hers sold electronics. On the giant screen television in the window, Trevor recognized Prince Nikolai giving a speech. The crawl under his picture said "Prince denounces Lukinburg terrorists. Secretary of Defense urges U.S. to step up plans to intervene."

Intervention. Terrorists. Regime change.

Words of war. With politicians and princes, it was too much talk and too little action. In Trevor's opinion, the way to handle this Lukinburg terrorist situation was not to deploy massive numbers of troops. All it took was one covert unit of Special Forces—a unit like the one formerly commanded by Cameron Murphy. These specialists could enter Lukinburg, assess the situation and, if possible, neutralize the terrorists.

As he stepped into the entryway of Olson's

Outdoor Sporting Goods, his cell phone rang. Though he could see Sierra staring at him from behind the counter, Trevor paused to answer.

It was Mike Clark. "Blackhaw, are you in Helena?"

"At the Galleria. What's up?"

"Lombardi and I turned up a lead and we need your interrogation skills. We're at the Sage Garden Shop."

Trevor knew the location. He'd driven past the place on his way into Helena this morning. "I'll be there in ten minutes."

He disconnected the call. He turned toward Sierra, who was coming toward him with a determined look in her eyes. No doubt she intended to give him another piece of her mind. Not this time.

He gave her a wink, turned on his boot heel and walked away. Finally, he had something useful to do.

IN A MOTEL ROOM at the outskirts of Helena, Boone Fowler listened to chatter from a police scanner while his men checked and rechecked their weapons.

So far, Boone had picked up nothing of interest on the radio scanner. It sounded like just another day. This wasn't going according to his plan. Sierra should have told somebody about his phone call. She should have summoned law enforcement, including the unknown men who had been pursuing the Militia and thwarting their previous efforts.

He turned off the scanner. The time had come for Boone to pump up his men, to fuel their eagerness.

"We're making a statement," he said. Shoulders back and chest out, he knew that he presented an imposing figure. "We're going to show the world that a well-trained band of men can outsmart and outmaneuver the cops, the feds and the National Guard."

A murmur went through the Militia. They were prepared for this assault. Thanks to financing from the Puppetmaster, they were well-equipped and armed to the teeth. Dressed entirely in black and wearing enough body armor to make them invincible, they were on the move.

"You know we're doing the right thing," Boone said. "Like the American patriots in the Revolution, we will show the corrupt U.S. government that we demand our God-given right to freedom. No more taxation. No more regulation. No more suppression."

Their gleaming eyes focused sharply on him. They were breathing heavily, anticipating the life-and-death assault that lay before them.

"This is a battle," Boone said. "We will avenge our fallen comrades. Men, are you with me?"

"Yes!"

"You have your assigned tasks. Perform them well."

"Yes."

"We are free men. Americans. Glorious and free. And we will succeed." His voice lowered. "Prepare yourselves for battle."

They gathered up their automatic weapons and

vests lined with explosives and pipe bombs. The Militia was ready to take on the world.

TREVOR ARRIVED at the gardening shop in a matter of minutes. He pulled into the parking lot beside Mike Clark's van and leaped from his Jeep. "What's up, Clark?"

"Lombardi and I were keeping an eye on this place. To see if any of the Militia were dumb enough to come shopping here for sodium nitrate and sulfur."

"Were they?"

"Somebody bought thirty bags of fertilizer."

"Militia?"

"Not exactly," Clark said with a grin. "But I think you're the right man to do this particular interrogation."

He slid open the door to a no-frills paneled van he used for hauling. There were no seats inside the flatbed, and the only light came from the front windows. Tony Lombardi crouched near the front seats. He held a gun on a man, who was gagged, his hands cuffed in front of him.

Trevor peered into the rear of the van and recognized Danny—the ringleader of the jerks who had come after Sierra at Lyle Nelson's funeral. "Well, well," Trevor said. "We meet again."

Danny's eyes got big. Apparently, he remembered the beating Trevor had given him. Because Danny was already intimidated, this interrogation ought to be a piece of cake.

Trevor nodded to Lombardi. "Leave me alone with this son of a bitch."

"I don't know, man." Lombardi played along, helping Trevor build on Danny's fear. "The last time we left you alone with a subject, the guy nearly died."

"I hear he committed suicide," Trevor said.

Behind the gag, Danny whimpered.

"Suicide, huh?" Lombardi shook his head. "I'm not surprised. You have a reputation as the toughest, most brutal interrogator ever trained by Special Forces."

"I earned that rep."

Lombardi gave their prisoner a pat on the shoulder. "Good luck, man."

When Lombardi left the van, Trevor removed his hat and climbed inside. In spite of what Lombardi had said about brutality, he seldom found it necessary to touch his interrogation subjects. The threat was enough.

Inhaling a sustained breath, he took on the attitude of an interrogator. He cleansed his mind of empathy, kindness and charity. There should be no evidence of softness or human emotion. The goal of interrogation was single-minded focus on obtaining accurate information.

When he turned his head and studied his subject, Trevor felt calm and controlled. "Look at me, Danny."

The other man shook his head. He sat cross-legged on the floor with his shoulders hunched, staring down at the handcuffs on his wrists.

Trevor hunkered down. He removed his jacket. In calm, deliberate movements, he unbuttoned his shirt cuffs and rolled up his sleeves. Though the subject was pretending not to watch, Trevor caught a flicker of a glance.

When Trevor slid the van door shut, Danny winced. The enclosed space was suddenly stifling, reeking with the odor of fear.

"Look at me," Trevor snapped.

The subject's head lifted. He met Trevor's blue-eyed gaze.

"That's good, Danny." He rewarded the subject with a cold, predatory smile—the look a boa constrictor might give to a mouse before swallowing it whole.

In seconds, Trevor had accomplished his first goal as an interrogator. He had obtained voluntary cooperation from his subject. "Keep looking right here. In my eyes."

Though Danny trembled, he maintained eye contact.

"The way I hear," Trevor said, "you bought thirty bags of fertilizer. That's a hell of a big gardening project."

He reached into his jacket pocket and pulled out a pair of black leather gloves. Carefully, he slipped them on and snapped his fingers into fists, allowing the subject to imagine what kind of damage those fists might inflict. "Fertilizer has a lot of uses. Thirty bags. That's enough to bury a man standing up. Can you picture that? Buried in fertilizer. That'd be a bad way to die. All those chemicals—sulfur and sodium nitrate—eating away at your flesh, burning through your eyelids. Eventually you'd suffocate, but it'd be slow. Real slow."

Trevor smacked his fist against the side of the van and the sound resonated. "Keep looking at me, Danny."

The subject's eyelids flapped like moth wings.

"Don't look away," Trevor growled. "Not unless I tell you to. Do you understand? Nod your head if you understand."

Danny's head went up and down.

"Good." Second step accomplished. The subject was agreeing with him.

Trevor took out his pocketknife. It was only a three inch blade, not particularly scary. But the polished steel gleamed with a dangerous light. He brought the razor-sharp blade close to the subject's face. With a flick of his wrist, he cut the bandanna that had been used as a gag.

"Take a breath, Danny."

The subject gasped. His skin was mottled. His greasy hair hung limp around his cheeks. "Don't hurt me, man. I don't want—"

"Shut up." Trevor leaned closer. His voice was a harsh whisper, meant to penetrate deeply into the subject's brain. "I'll ask the questions. You answer. Nod if you understand."

Another vigorous nod.

"You bought that fertilizer for the Militia," Trevor said.

"That's right. I got a phone call and they told me where to go and what to buy."

"Where are they? Where's the hideout?"

"I don't know."

"Tell me."

"Really, man. I don't know."

Trevor toyed with his knife. He balanced the blade at eye level, maintaining the threat. But he didn't think Danny was lying. His panicky denial came too quickly. Also, Trevor couldn't imagine Boone Fowler being foolish enough to trust this low-level underling with important information.

"Where," Trevor said, "were you supposed to deliver the fertilizer?"

"They said they'd contact me."

Unfortunately, that made sense. But why had the Militia told Danny to come to this particular shop? There was something else going on. "Boone Fowler is an organized man. What exactly did Boone tell you to do?"

"Come to this shop. Buy the fertilizer and wait until it all got loaded into my truck."

"Did he give you a time?"

Danny nodded. "Half past eleven. But I got here early, so I just went ahead and did it."

This sounded like a setup. Boone must have

guessed that gardening shops would be under surveillance. Maybe Danny was meant to be a distraction. From what?

Danny leaned toward him. "Listen, I know you're not really a cop. You could let me go and—"

"Shut up." Trevor's face was inches away from the subject. "You don't tell me to listen. You don't tell me anything. Understand? Nod for yes."

When Danny bobbed his head, his chin wobbled.

Trevor sat back on his heels. There was something odd about this interrogation. The subject had offered little resistance. He seemed too anxious to spill his guts. "If you want me to let you free, Danny, you've got to give me something."

"They're making bombs."

"Tell me more."

"They're planning something big. A brave and gallant statement. The Militia is going to show the whole world that a small band of highly trained patriots can take on all the law enforcement in Montana."

Trevor recognized the sick rhetoric of Boone Fowler. Danny's rote repetition of his leader's words were obscene. This little worm had no mind of his own. "That's a pretty big goal. Taking on all the law enforcement in Montana. When's this supposed to happen?"

His lips pressed together. He looked like a kid with a secret that he couldn't wait to tell.

Trevor gave him a little reverse-psychology nudge.

"Never mind, Danny. You probably don't know. Boone Fowler wouldn't trust somebody like you with that information."

"It's now," Danny blurted. A feverish excitement trembled through him. "Before noon. Right now. At the Galleria."

Trevor hid his shock behind a sneer. A bomb at the mall? He'd explored that two-story structure. Though the construction was solid concrete, well-placed explosions could create structural devastation and fire. There would be casualties. Innocent victims…like Sierra.

"You're lying, Danny."

"Hell, no. I'm not."

"If the Militia already has a bomb, why did they send you to buy fertilizer?"

"There's going to be other stuff."

"Other bombs?"

"That's right," he said quickly. "This is just the start of a big operation."

"Too bad you won't be around to enjoy the explosions."

It was time to conclude this interrogation. Trevor whipped open the van door and leaped out. He summoned Lombardi and Clark with a quick gesture. "Here's the deal. Danny says there's a bomb at the Galleria. It's supposed to detonate before noon."

"What else?" Clark asked.

"This feels like a setup." If Trevor had had more

time to spend interrogating Danny, he would have squeezed out every detail. "But we can't take the chance that it isn't. Tell the other bounty hunters that we need backup at the mall. Notify the police and turn this scum over to them."

"Where are you going?"

"To the Galleria."

Sierra was there. She stood directly in harm's way.

Chapter Seven

At Olson's Outdoor Sporting Goods, Sierra tidied up the shoe display area and straightened the tags indicating inventory markdowns to make way for the Christmas stock. Thursdays tended to be slow, especially in the morning, and she was alone in the store, which gave her too much time to worry. She should have told someone about the phone call from Boone. If not the cops, she should have told Trevor. He claimed to be one of the good guys. Maybe he could have figured out a way to notify the authorities without dragging her through the muck and mire of suspicion.

Should have told him... Should have... Should have... If that slimeball Boone Fowler sneaked in and out of the mall without being nabbed by the cops, she'd never forgive herself.

She glanced toward the front of the store. Where was Trevor? All week long, he'd been on her tail. And now when she wanted him, he was nowhere to be found. Typical male.

Nobody else was here, either. Her manager had taken an early lunch at eleven o'clock. Before he left, they had been discussing seasonal displays. Since it was October, Sierra wanted to drape orange and black crepe paper around the store. Then they could paint jack-o-lantern pumpkin faces on the Day-Glo-orange hunting vests worn by employees as a uniform. The manager disagreed. According to him, sporting goods didn't lend themselves to Halloween unless trick-or-treating qualified as a sport.

As she stood with a running shoe in one hand, she saw Trevor loping through the mall with long-legged strides. If he was trying for subtlety in his surveillance, he'd just flunked. A tall, handsome, half-Cherokee cowboy racing through a mall tended to attract attention.

She grinned. Though he was jogging in hat and boots, Trevor somehow managed to maintain his cool. Everything he did, every move he made, seemed calculated and precise. Even when he'd mistakenly given her beef, he'd made crestfallen look good.

Entering the store, he grasped her hand. "Come with me. Now."

"I can't leave." She smacked the heel of the sneaker against his hand. "I'm working."

"The Militia has planned an attack on the mall. A bomb. You need to get the hell out of here."

"A bomb?" Her petty worries vanished in the face of this larger threat. "How do you know?"

"I'll explain later."

She shook her head in denial. Boone Fowler and the Militia were dangerous, no doubt about that. But how could these ragtag fugitives find the wherewithal to organize a bomb attack? "You're mistaken."

"I wish I was." His lips thinned in a straight, determined line. Nothing in his expression or manner indicated doubt. He believed this threat to be true.

"A bomb," she whispered.

Outside her store, she saw pedestrians. Mothers pushing strollers. Office workers on their lunch hour. Older folks who walked inside to avoid the vagaries of October weather. If Trevor was right, their peaceful world was about to be shattered.

She stepped briskly to the front of the store. Glancing toward the exit to the parking lot, she saw a group of firefighters in full regalia pushing through the doors. From the streets outside, she heard the muffled screams of approaching sirens. Something terrible was about to happen.

Trevor took her elbow. "Keep moving. Let's get out of here."

"Wait." She planted herself. "There must be some way I can help."

"Don't be crazy, Sierra. You can't stop a bomb explosion."

Fighting her rising fear, she stared into his intense blue eyes. "You've been keeping surveillance on me ever since Lyle's funeral. Why? Because you think the Militia wants revenge on me. Am I right?"

"Yes."

"And now there's a bomb at the place where I work. Coincidence?"

"I don't believe in coincidence," he said.

"Neither do I." She'd been a fool not to report the call from Boone Fowler. "This is my fault."

"Yeah, and we'll talk about it later. Right now I need to get you the hell away from here."

He was right. Only a fool would stand in the path of a terrorist attack. "Let me grab my purse from the storeroom. Then we're out of here."

He followed her to the rear of the store.

In the mall the public address system blasted a warning squawk followed by instructions. "This is an emergency. Proceed in an orderly fashion to the nearest exit. This is not a drill."

In the storage area behind the sporting goods store, she went into an office cubicle and opened the closet door. As she grabbed her jacket and her backpack, her hands trembled. She sensed the nearness of danger. *This is not a drill.*

There was a loud crash from the back of the storage room, punctuated by gunfire.

"What's back there?" Trevor demanded.

"Loading dock. The door is always locked."

"Not anymore."

He rushed her away from the office into the store.

The exit to the mall seemed a million miles away. If armed men had broken through the rear door, she and Trevor would never make it to the exit in time. They'd be gunned down. Shot in the back.

"Over here." She pulled him toward the sales counter behind the cash register. Together they ducked down.

Trevor had unholstered his automatic pistol, but she was unarmed. The glass display case for hunting rifles was behind the counter within easy reach. There was enough weaponry here to arm a small army. Is that why the Militia had chosen to come through her store? For more weapons?

Another blast of gunfire echoed from the rear of the storage area.

Beside her, Trevor stood. Using the butt of his automatic pistol, he broke the glass on the display case and opened the latch.

"What are you doing?" she whispered.

"Arming myself."

"Give me a rifle."

"Do you know how to shoot?"

"Lyle taught me."

With the rifle in her hand, she felt less vulnerable but no less scared. It took all her concentration to open the ammunition drawer and load the twelve-gauge.

From the storeroom, a group of heavily armed men dressed in black charged into the display and sales area. They seemed to be covered in protective padding and wore the kind of helmets used by SWAT teams.

"Two minutes," shouted one of the men.

"I heard you," said their leader. "Loud and clear."

Sierra recognized the voice of the leader. It was not Boone Fowler, but Perry Johnson. Terror overwhelmed her. Perry would rather shoot her than look at her. She tried to aim her rifle, peering through the sight. Her vision blurred.

"Don't shoot," Trevor whispered urgently. "They're wearing explosive vests."

She lifted her trigger finger.

"I'll aim low," he said. She watched as he squeezed off a shot.

PERRY FELT A SHARP THUD against the Kevlar armor covering his thigh. He'd heard a shot; the sound came from the direction of the cash register. He turned and saw two rifle bores aimed directly at him.

"Scatter." He yelled the command to his men. "We've got gunmen."

But one of them was a woman. Sierra Collins. That bitch was shooting at him. Perry lowered his automatic rifle and sprayed the wooden counter with bullets.

This wasn't the way their assault was supposed to go. The timing was off.

He and his men were supposed to burst into the sporting goods store, where he would have the pleasure of killing Sierra face-to-face. He'd looked forward to seeing the fear in her eyes, maybe hearing her beg for her life. And then, kapow! She'd be dead.

In the next phase of their plan, he and his men would enter the mall, grab hostages and retreat back into this store to wait until Boone gave them the word to execute the final action.

Instead, Sierra was armed and shooting at him.

"Perry," called Marcus Smith, the explosives expert. "We've only got forty-five seconds."

There wasn't time to kill Sierra. Enraged, Perry unleashed another blast at the counter. Then he gestured for his men to go forward. "Move out."

Perry swiveled his head from side to side. How the hell could he think clearly with this helmet restricting his field of vision? All this body armor and the explosive vest weighed him down.

Before they entered the mall, Raymond Fleming darted up beside him. "What are we supposed to do now?"

"Five seconds," Marcus said.

Perry had to make a couple of adjustments in their original plan. He could do it. He would not fail.

"Two seconds," Marcus said.

Perry braced himself.

The explosion of the heavy-duty C-4 explosives on a timer in the food court pounded the concrete structure of the Galleria with a satisfying blast, followed by screams and shouts and the stink of destruction.

It was beautiful.

SIERRA PRESSED HER BACK against the counter. She was unharmed, and she had Trevor to thank. An instant before Perry had squeezed off a round of automatic gunfire, Trevor had pulled her down flat on the floor.

Her eyelids pressed shut as echoes from the explosion rolled over her. Her fingers tensed on the cold metal of the rifle.

Beside her on the floor, Trevor spoke into his cell phone. "The Militia entered through the sporting goods store. Lower level. Near the west entrance. They're wearing explosive vests. Instruct the other officers. Don't shoot. Repeat. Don't shoot."

He disconnected the call and turned toward her. "You okay?"

"I think so."

"You did good, Sierra. You make a good partner."

"Not really. I didn't even fire my rifle."

"Moral support is everything." He gave her a wink and rose to his feet. "The next thing I want you to do is stay here and don't get shot."

"What if they come back this way."

Rifle in hand, he strode toward the front of the store. "They won't come back."

But what if they did? She certainly didn't want to be stuck here behind the counter by herself. Escaping through the rear exit didn't seem like a good alternative, since that was the route the Militia had used to enter.

Instinctively she knew that the safest place she

could be was beside Trevor. She stood and hurried through the display racks to the entrance that led to the mall.

Just outside the store she saw the band of Militia. They seemed to be rounding up pedestrians, including women and children. "What are they doing?"

He frowned at her. "I thought I told you to—"

"I'd rather be here with you. Why are they grabbing those people?"

"Taking hostages," Trevor said. He stood tall and took aim, but he didn't fire. "There are too many people. I can't get a clear shot."

Frustration boiled inside him as he lowered his rifle. The Militia had thought of everything to protect themselves. Exploding vests. Body armor and helmets. Now hostages. But why? What the hell did they hope to accomplish with this action?

The only way Trevor could find out was to take one of them down and ask questions. He moved into the open so he'd have a better shot. Sierra was right behind him.

"Taking hostages is wrong," she said. "They're only kids. They must be scared to death."

"Damn it, Sierra. Get back inside the store."

"Where are the firemen? And the cops?"

"They must have gone toward the explosion."

"I guess that leaves you and me to stop these guys." She raised her rifle. "Partner."

"Those vests are packed with explosives," he warned her. "Aim for their ankles."

"Got it."

"Don't shoot if there's a hostage in the way."

"Right."

He had to admire her grit, her selfless bravery. Sierra would have made a good soldier.

Sighting down the barrel of his rifle, Trevor tried again to get a clean shot. It was impossible. The people in the mall who weren't being grabbed as hostages fled wildly. One woman, bleeding from a head wound, collapsed on the floor.

Trevor took aim at the lower legs of the man who appeared to be the leader. A child darted in front of him. Holding the little boy, the leader raised his automatic weapon to return fire. But he wasn't aiming at Trevor. Sierra! She stood right beside him.

Without thinking, Trevor reacted. He dived toward her, knocking her off her feet. Holding her tightly, he rolled back inside the store and found cover.

He pulled her up to a kneeling position, quickly inspecting her. "Are you okay?"

"I dropped my rifle."

"Let's get it."

But when they peered into the mall again, the Militia were gone. They had retreated into the electronics store next door to Olson's Outdoor Sporting Goods. And, Trevor knew, they had taken the hostages with them.

"We're too late."

The need for action still pulsed in his veins, but he knew this battle was over. And the Militia had won. Inside the sporting goods store he sprawled on the floor with Sierra beside him, his arm wrapped around her shoulders.

"What will they do?"

"Since they have hostages, I assume there will be demands."

"For money?"

He doubted this assault was about raising capital. If they wanted cash, they would have gone to a bank. Besides, they were outfitted smartly, with expensive weaponry. Unless Trevor missed his guess, somebody else was footing the bill for the Militia. "It's likely that they have some kind of statement. This bomb blast and coordinated assault was a show of power."

"There's got to be something else we can do." Her copper-blond hair fell across her forehead as she lowered her head. "I don't want to give up."

"We tried."

"It's not good enough." When she looked up at him, her eyes brimmed with tears. "This is my fault, Trevor. Boone Fowler called me on Monday and threatened to come to the Galleria. I should have told someone."

"You're right. You should have told me."

A sob racked her shoulders. "I never thought of

a bomb, never thought he meant to hurt anybody but me."

Trevor pulled her close. Her body trembled against his chest. Though she needed his reassurance, he wouldn't lie to her. "Let's try to figure this out. In that phone call, what did Boone say? Exact words."

"He said he had money for me. Lyle's share of something. Then he said I would get what I deserved."

Sitting on the floor of the sporting goods store, Trevor stroked Sierra's back. For days he'd been trying to get this lovely woman into his arms, but this wasn't what he wanted. Not tears. Not this miserable sense of failure.

"We're not giving up," he said.

"Good." She took a deep breath, then another. It seemed she was gathering her strength. "What should we do?"

"Let me think."

The bomb in the Galleria and the armed assault had been carefully planned. Therefore, he had to assume that the phone call to Sierra wasn't random. How did the phone call serve the purposes of the Militia? "When Boone called you, what did he expect you to do?"

"He probably thought I'd call the cops."

"And the response from law enforcement would have been to question you and to place a few more cops in the Galleria."

"Doesn't make sense." She leaned away and swiped the tears from her cheeks. "Why would he want to alert the police?"

"A trap." Trevor thought of Danny at the garden shop. Danny, the Militia sympathizer, had been too anxious to spill his guts. "It was a setup. Boone wanted to lure law enforcement to the mall."

"Why?"

"He wants everybody who might be pursuing him to be here." Trevor frowned as the last logical piece clicked into place. Boone had enacted an old and not particularly sophisticated battle plan. He wanted to bring all his enemies together in one place. Then he would attack. "The Militia is going to use potassium cyanide to wipe out as many officers as possible."

And bounty hunters. Boone Fowler held a long-standing grudge against Cameron Murphy.

Sierra gazed up into his eyes. "So, this wasn't about me?"

"Killing you was a bonus. That's why they entered the Galleria through the back of your store."

"Thank God!" She clutched her hands to her chest. "It wouldn't have mattered if I told the police."

"You're not off the hook," he said. "You should have told me about the contact."

"You're right, Trevor. No more secrets." She smiled up at him. "Can we still be partners?"

"I'd like to be the man who protects your back."

"Same here."

She wrapped her arms around him, and he embraced her. The barrier between them had crumbled. From now on, they were on the same side.

Chapter Eight

Sierra stood at the second-floor railing beside Trevor and looked down at the devastation caused by the Militia's bomb explosion in the Galleria food court. Her favorite lunch table beside the wall of windows had been obliterated.

Those tall windows were shattered. Shards of glass sparkled amid the scorched wreckage, which was now being searched by firefighters and forensic investigators. Why investigate? It was obvious what had happened. The Militia had happened. And they needed to pay.

Anger churned inside her. She raised her hand to cover her mouth, and pinched her nostrils shut against the noxious stench of charred metal, concrete and plastic.

The food shops that lined the edge of the court were gaping holes. Their signs and counters were burned beyond recognition, their food-processing equipment mangled. The tables and chairs in the food court had scattered in a chaotic pattern that radiated out from a center support beam. The bomb must have been planted there. She eyed the thick concrete pillar that rose from floor to ceiling. If it had collapsed, the roof of the Galleria would have caved. The devastation would have been worse. "It's hard to believe nobody was killed."

"There were injuries," Trevor said grimly.

He had been on his cell phone frequently, gathering information. Thus far, he had learned that the Militia had taken ten hostages. Their demands included a million dollars and a helicopter. They also had a statement—a videotape of Boone Fowler that they wanted played on television.

"Who's this person you keep talking to on the cell phone?" she asked.

"Cameron Murphy. He was my commanding officer when I was in the Special Forces, and he was largely responsible for the capture of Boone Fowler and the Militia the last time they were apprehended."

"So he's got credibility," she concluded. "That's important. It means the police will listen to him."

Trevor took off his hat and raked his fingers through his shiny black hair. He looked different. Intense.

After that brief moment of reconciliation when she'd wept in his arms, he'd gone into action, his focus narrowed to a laser point. A fierce intensity flamed in his keen blue eyes. Every muscle in his body was taut.

As she studied him, Sierra realized that she was being given a glimpse into Trevor Blackhaw's true nature. He had told her that he was a bounty hunter and an interrogator. But she saw something deeper in him, an almost primal identity. Above all else, he was a warrior, a man who lived to fight the good fight. He would show no mercy to his enemies, and he would defend the innocent with his last breath.

She was proud to be his partner.

Trevor turned his head, alert to a sound she hadn't even heard. "Here's Murphy now."

It was no surprise to her that Cameron Murphy was another formidable man. Probably about forty, he had black hair, dark eyes and an indefinable air of authority.

He shook her hand as he identified himself. Then he turned toward Trevor. "You said there was something important you needed to tell me."

"This is a setup," Trevor said. "The explosion. The Militia in explosive vests. The taking of hostages. It's all a ploy."

"How so?"

"Boone Fowler has put a plan in motion that will guarantee the presence of every law enforcement person in the state of Montana—everybody who's after the Militia. All his enemies."

"A classic military strategy," Cameron said.

"With all these people—including the bounty hunters—gathered in one place, Boone Fowler will detonate explosives to disperse the nerve gas. In one action, he will disable many of his pursuers."

Murphy gave a curt nod. "You're onto something."

"I strongly advise," Trevor said, "that most of the FBI, SWAT teams, sheriffs and police be evacuated. Those who stay should be equipped with gas masks."

"Which aren't a guarantee against exposure," Murphy said. "Potassium cyanide can be absorbed through the skin. Anything else?"

"You should be the first person to leave, sir. The Militia has a serious resentment toward you."

When Murphy grinned, Sierra saw a reflection of the same warrior spirit she had seen in Trevor. Formidable men, indeed.

"I won't retreat," Murphy said. "Not if I'm the target that will draw Boone Fowler into the open."

"Boone's not here," Sierra said. "He wasn't leading the attack team. That was Perry Johnson."

"He's here," Murphy said. "I feel it in my bones."

A crackle came over the public address system in the Galleria, and Sierra glanced up. She was amazed that the system was still working.

The announcement sounded surprisingly distinct. "The hostage takers demand that we play the following audio."

Boone Fowler's harsh baritone resonated over the destruction his Militia had caused. "We are the true patriots, unafraid to stand up for what we believe. We are willing to become terrorists in order to save our once proud nation."

Trevor reacted with a frown. "That's a change in his usual line of crap—the mention of terrorism."

Cameron nodded. "Boone doesn't usually align himself with the other terrorists of the world. He likes to think the Militia is unique."

"Bastards," Sierra muttered. "The only difference between the Militia and a gang of schoolyard bullies is that they have better weapons."

"Unfortunately," Cameron said, "their weapons are life-threatening. I'd like to see you and Trevor get out of here. Out of harm's way."

As Boone's voice continued with his illogical rhetoric—condemning capitalism with one breath and demanding a million dollars with the next—the rage inside her built. "I won't leave until I see the Militia captured. Or dead."

"I've heard about your stubbornness," Cameron said. "Be careful, Sierra."

"I will be."

He turned to Trevor. "I'll put forward your theory, but I can't promise to make a difference. It's going to take some tough talk to get all these high-ranking law enforcement people to agree on a course of action."

"I understand."

Cameron looked back toward Sierra. "Any chance you'll change your mind and get out of here?"

"No, sir."

"You don't intend to listen to reason?"

She shook her head. "Nope."

With a grin, he nodded to her and then to Trevor. "Good luck."

Cameron strode toward the center of operations, where law enforcement officials had gathered. Though Trevor didn't actually salute when his former commander walked away, his posture stiffened. His respect for Cameron Murphy was obvious.

"He's right," Trevor said. "We should go."

"I won't give up."

"Believe me, Sierra. I don't like the idea any more than you do."

In his voice, she heard his deep frustration. In his clenched fist, she saw barely checked rage. This was not a man who liked to retreat. "There might be something we can do."

"Such as?"

"Rescue the hostages."

"Just like that?" He snapped his fingers. "There are probably a hundred cops, FBI and SWAT assault teams swarming all over this mall. The electronics store where the hostages are being held is surrounded, but you think you can waltz right in and save them."

"I know a few things the SWAT teams don't." For several months, she had worked next door to the electronics store where the hostages were being held. "For one thing, I'm familiar with the ins and outs of the ventilation system."

He eyed her curiously. "May I ask why you know this?"

"Long story short," she said. "There was a hamster escape in the pet store. Somebody had to volunteer to look for the little beasts. So I went on a search, crawling through the air ducts."

"You're a strange woman, Sierra."

"And a determined one." If there was anything she could do to thwart the Militia, she had to try. "I can't just step back and let these slimeballs hurt innocent women and children. Come on, Trevor. I don't want to run and hide."

"It's not like that," he said. "We're stepping back and letting all these lawmen do their jobs."

"What if we can do it better?" She could see him leaning in her direction. In his heart, he wanted to go on the attack. She made a last appeal to his warrior spirit. "We can fight the Militia. And we will win. Are you with me, partner?"

He gave a quick nod. "All the way."

WHEN TREVOR AGREED to go along with Sierra, he didn't really expect they'd be allowed access to the sporting goods store. The situation in the Galleria bordered on chaos, but security had tightened. The authorities would never allow him and Sierra to attempt their own rescue of the hostages.

Nonetheless, they came up with a plan. The first step was to get close to the sporting goods store.

Trevor wished he had backup from the other bounty hunters. Since Murphy was here, he assumed the other men were busy with their own missions using their special expertise. He had no assignment. In a situation like this, there wasn't much call for an interrogator.

He and Sierra approached command central for law enforcement a group that now included Cameron Murphy. These men had taken a strategic position on the second floor, directly across from the electronics store where the hostages were being held. Their location underlined the irony of a commando attack at a shopping mall; the store occupied by command central was Victoria's Secret—a place where few of these hard-boiled men had ever gone before.

Amid bras, panties and a whole bunch of pink lotions, orders were issued to the SWAT team sharpshooters. An intense FBI contingent worked on hostage negotiations. Other cops were deployed to clear all the cars from the parking lot and to deal with the media.

After an introduction from Murphy, Trevor faced off with the county sheriff, an elected official who was famous for being an outdoorsman.

Trevor stated his request. "We need a couple of deputies to evacuate the pet store."

The sheriff raised both bushy eyebrows. "Come again?"

"If nerve gas is released in the Galleria, those animals will die."

"Listen up," the sheriff growled. "We've got a genuine crisis here. Human beings are in danger. We can't be worried about puppies and kitty cats."

His response was what Trevor had expected. "I understand, but—"

"Voters love puppies," Sierra interrupted. "The voting public would be really upset if they knew you abandoned a pet store. You can't let those animals die."

The sheriff frowned and rubbed at his neatly trimmed beard as he considered her words.

"You know I'm right," Sierra continued. "If one fluffy Persian kitty is overcome by nerve gas, you can kiss the little-old-lady vote goodbye.

With an impatient gesture, the sheriff summoned three deputies and gave the order. "Evacuate the damn pet store. And make sure the media people see you carrying puppies out of the mall."

Sierra led the way across the upper level and down an escalator to the pet shop, which was on the first floor and around a corner from the electronics store. While the deputies opened cages and picked up animals, she took Trevor to the back of the place, near the fish tanks. She pointed to the ventilation shaft. "If we climb through here, we can get to my store."

When she loosened the screws on the grate covering the air duct, Trevor peered into the narrow opening. His throat clenched. He couldn't go in there. The mere thought of that tightly enclosed space made him want to puke. "I've got another idea."

She glanced up at him. Her dark eyes were bright and excited. "Tell me."

"We can go through the corridors behind the stores. The shipping dock area." His gaze fastened on the tiny air duct. It seemed to shrink before his eyes. He'd rather fight a hundred armed terrorists than enter that tight space. "We can reach the sporting goods store the same way the Militia did. Through the rear."

"It would be a lot easier that way," she said. "But I'm sure the SWAT guys are back there. Do you think they'll let us through?"

"Worth a try." He turned away from the shaft. "We'll take a couple of puppies."

With basset hound puppies under each arm, Trevor exited through the back of the store. Sierra was right behind him, carrying more puppies.

Even the windowless concrete corridor that ran behind the shops felt too claustrophobic for Trevor. He gulped down a couple of breaths, struggling against the tension that coiled inside his belly like a sleeping rattlesnake.

He marched past the SWAT team sharpshooters with a quiet explanation. "We're evacuating the pet store."

Behind their face shields, each of the men nodded in understanding. And they smiled at the wriggling dogs. Apparently puppies were a passport to anywhere.

At the rear of the sporting goods store, he and

Sierra made a quick turn. The lock on the rear door had been blown with excessive force, demolishing half the wall beside it.

They were inside.

"So far, so good," Trevor said.

"What do we do with these little guys?" Sierra lowered her face for a sloppy kiss from a chocolate-brown poodle with big luminous eyes.

As Trevor watched her interact with the pooch, he had to wonder how he had gotten himself into this position. He was partners with a vegetarian crazy lady from Brooklyn. And they were going up against dangerous men who were in possession of lethal nerve gas.

His weapon? Puppies.

He strode toward a small office with a door. "Put the dogs in here."

"They're going to make a mess on the floor."

He glared at her. Obviously Sierra had lost her mind. "This is a life-and-death situation. Not the time to worry about puppy poop."

"We should get the doggies out of here. If the nerve gas is dispersed, they'll be killed."

"And so will we," he pointed out. "Let's try to focus, Sierra."

They closed the door on the puppies, and she led him to the rear of the crowded storeroom. Her voice dropped to a whisper. "Back here, there's only a wall dividing our stockroom from the other store."

"What kind of wall?"

"It's not very thick," she said. "Olson's Outdoor Sporting Goods used to own both spaces, then they divided it up and the electronics business moved in."

"Tell me about the setup in the electronics store."

"It's the same as here. Showroom in front. Stockroom in back."

It seemed logical that the Militia would keep their hostages locked in a back room where they wouldn't get in the way. But was there a Militia guard watching them?

Moving as a team, Trevor and Sierra cleared away the stacks of sporting equipment until they had an open space of wall. He pressed his ear against the drywall and listened. He distinctly heard conversation. A whimper. A gasping sob. "They're back here."

"How do we get them out?"

They needed to make a hole in the wall to see if there was a guard. Trevor had the feeling they should move fast. He glanced at his wristwatch. An hour had elapsed since the assault on the sporting goods store. "We'd better hurry."

"Why? The Militia knows it's going to take some time to put together the helicopter and ransom money."

"Or maybe not. We can't take the chance that they'll wait."

With the tip of his pocketknife, he carved a hole in the wall on the sporting goods side. The plaster crumbled easily. Sierra had been right. The walls separating these stores were insubstantial—nothing more than thin drywall on either side, with one-by-three supports every eighteen inches. He whispered, "I need something to make a hole we can see through."

She rifled through equipment and came up with a ski pole.

Gently, he pushed the tip of the pole through the wall. It made a circular spot for viewing. When Trevor peered through, he was looking through shelving stacked with boxes. He could see the hostages—women and children huddled together, There was no sign of a guard.

DISGUISED IN THE GEAR of a SWAT sharpshooter, Boone Fowler had positioned himself on the Galleria's second floor. From this angle, he could see directly into the command center in Victoria's Secret.

Eight minutes ago, he'd spotted Sierra and a tall guy who looked part-Indian talking to the county sheriff. Who was that half-breed? Could he be the man responsible for disrupting the Militia's other attacks?

When they'd headed to the pet store, they had passed within ten feet of Boone. He had been sorely tempted to shoot Sierra Collins then and there. The woman was a thorn in his side. Thanks to her interference, his men were holed up in the electronics store instead of in sporting goods.

His fingers had tensed on the automatic rifle he held in his gloved hands, but he had managed to curb his instinct for revenge. Sierra would die—like everybody else—when the potassium cyanide was dispersed.

The Militia assault had not gone precisely according to Boone's plans. First, there'd been the confusion in the sporting goods store. Perry's quick thinking had saved that situation. Then the bomb in the food court failed to demolish the center support beam, and firefighters had managed to contain the blaze too easily.

Rising disappointment fed Boone's impatience. More than once he told himself to calm down. Though the destruction was far less than he'd hoped for, this action wasn't a total failure.

The taking of hostages assured that media attention would be widespread and in-depth. In Boone's televised statement, he'd made sure to mention terrorism. The Puppetmaster ought to be pleased about that. And there was still opportunity for large scale devastation to humans.

He permitted himself a cold smile. The lethal nerve gas would guarantee fatalities. The hostages would die. That much was damn certain. And the sheriff, the feds and the cops who had gathered in command central would be affected in spite of their gas masks.

He stared back into the lingerie shop where they were huddled. And then Boone saw what he was looking for. Cameron Murphy.

There was no man on earth he hated more than Cameron Murphy. Because of him, the Militia had been apprehended and thrown into the Fortress. Because of him, the alliance with the Puppetmaster was necessary. Surely, Cameron Murphy had to be the person who had foiled the previous Militia actions.

A uniformed deputy came up beside Boone. He paused and asked, "Is this your position?"

"That's right," Boone said, confident that the face shield would make identification impossible. "Any new developments?"

"Nothing I know about."

Boone nodded toward command central, using this unwitting deputy to get more intelligence about Cameron Murphy. "Who's that guy with the cowboy hat? The one talking to the sheriff."

"Former military," the deputy said. "He's a bounty hunter now. From what I hear, he's got a team that works with him. Big Sky Bounty Hunters. These guys were handpicked from Special Forces."

"Looks like all the law enforcement personnel in the state of Montana are here," Boone said.

"Just about." The deputy touched the brim of his hat and moved on. "Good luck."

"Same to you."

Big Sky Bounty Hunters. Finally, Boone had a name for his nemesis. Better yet, he had them right where he wanted them. In the line of fire.

He raised the walkie-talkie to his mouth, flipped

the communication switch and contacted Perry. "Initiate final action. Five minutes."

As soon as Trevor ascertained that the hostages were unguarded, he had called to them and warned them to move quietly so the Militia wouldn't be alerted. There were eleven people packed into the crowded stockroom of the electronics store. One older man. Six women—four adults and two teenagers. And four children.

The hostages worked from their side to move stock away from the wall so they could make a hole and escape. At the same time, Trevor and Sierra chipped away at the plaster separating the two stockrooms.

He knew how risky it was to attempt this rescue. If the Militia discovered their scheme, they wouldn't hesitate to kill one or more of the hostages. They'd already proved themselves to be ruthless.

"Quietly," he told them. "Move very quietly. But fast."

Trevor wouldn't expect a medal for this action. The fact that the FBI negotiators had not initiated a rescue attempt indicated that they'd been warned or threatened.

"Are we doing the right thing?" Sierra whispered. Her breath was hot in his ear.

He nodded. The fact that the Militia wasn't bothering to guard these people made him even more certain that the hostages meant nothing to them. Their goal was to release the nerve gas and kill lawmen. These people locked in the stockroom were nothing more than collateral. "Keep at it, Sierra."

Soon they had a hole the size of a doggy door. The four children came through. All of them were obviously terrified, silent with shock. Traumatized.

"Sierra, get the kids out of here," Trevor ordered.

"Right." She turned to the children. "Follow me."

"No." In a wavering voice, a little girl dared to resist. "I won't leave without my mommy."

"Hush now," Sierra whispered. "Your mommy is going to be fine. Right now, I have an important job for you. We need to take care of some puppies."

As she led them away, Trevor continued to chip at the wall. The hole needed to be considerably larger for the adults to fit through.

The danger was imminent. He could feel it in the prickling of the hairs on the back of his neck. At any second, the door to the stockroom could swing open and one of the Militia might march through.

Trevor instructed the hostages. "Move something in front of the door so nobody can get in."

The teenagers, who probably spent more time at the mall than was good for them, sprang into action. They shoved a couple of cardboard crates in front of the doorway.

Trevor motioned to one of the adults. "Come on. Shoulders first. I'll help you."

As she wedged her way through, into his arms, Trevor heard someone behind him. He turned and faced the deputies who had helped in the puppy evacuation. "Give me a hand," he said. "Let's get these people out of here."

With three of them working on the wall, the hole widened quickly. The hostages were free.

Instead of weaving through the concrete corridors behind the stores, Trevor escorted his little band to the front of the shop and out through the mall.

As the last teenage hostage raced out the glass doors to the safety of the parking lot, he heard a commotion from the electronics store. Standing just outside the mall, Trevor witnessed the final assault through the glass doors.

A smoke bomb exploded. Through the whirling smoke, five Militia men rushed into the Galleria. All of them wore gas masks. In a synchronized motion, they whipped off their vests and threw them to the floor.

Simultaneous explosions made a blinding flash.

Immediately the Militia retreated. Their mission had been accomplished.

Trevor stepped back, putting distance between himself and the Galleria. He knew the purpose of the detonation. Lethal nerve gas had been released into the air. Those who were exposed would start with coughing. Their throats would close. Their flesh would itch and burn like fire. Their eyes would be blinded. And then death.

There was nothing Trevor could do to save Cameron Murphy.

Chapter Nine

Sierra had some reservations about returning to the secluded log headquarters of Big Sky Bounty Hunters. It was here, in the basement level interrogation room, that Trevor had tied her to a chair and asked all those questions that she still couldn't quite remember. That day had been less than a week ago, but it seemed like ancient history.

So much had changed. The hovering possibility of danger had become a cruel reality. People had died at the Galleria. The current body count was seven. All of them were lawmen or firefighters. Over twenty-five others, including Cameron, were in the hospital, being treated for exposure to potassium cyanide.

Sierra could no longer pretend that she was capable of facing the Militia all by herself. And luckily, she didn't have to. She and Trevor were partners.

In the barn behind the headquarters, she sat on a rough wooden bench and leaned back against the barn wall, watching as he tended the horses. Trevor worked hard, mucking out the stalls with a pitchfork, tossing hay, checking the feed. So much energy! She had the sense that he was burning off leftover adrenaline from today's battle.

Though the barn was chilly, with both doors open to the afternoon sun, he stripped down to his sleeveless white undershirt. In spite of her exhaustion, Sierra sat up and took notice. How could she not? This was a fine view—one she hadn't seen before, but had imagined. Trevor had a long, lean body with arms nicely muscled from biceps to wrist. The sunlight glistened on his bronze shoulders and his long black hair, which was tied back in a ponytail at his nape. What would it be like to tangle her fingers in his hair? To caress those tight muscles? To feel that muscular torso pressed against her body?

For a long time after she lost her baby, Sierra had felt dead inside. It wasn't so much a depression as an overwhelming sadness. There were weeks when she didn't leave her bed. Days when she sat and stared, her mind a blank. During that period she could barely manage a conversation with the clerk at the supermarket, much less think about a relationship. Men were the very last thing on her mind.

Though she'd finally managed to drag herself out of the house and go to work, she was still wary. Men would ask her out, and she'd push them away. Nobody seemed worth the trouble.

Until now, she hadn't missed the contact. Until

now, she hadn't known Trevor. Watching him was sheer pleasure. Half of her brain warned her to stay away from him; a relationship could only bring trouble and pain. The other half urged her to pounce on this gorgeous man. No pain, no gain. Did she dare take the risk?

The chocolate-brown poodle puppy she'd rescued from the mall bounced across the stable and hopped up on the bench beside her. She scooped him onto her lap. Snuggling with the warm, furry animal reminded her that sometimes risks paid off.

All the hostages had survived. If she and Trevor hadn't undertaken their risky rescue, those people surely would have perished, and the fatalities at the Galleria would have been much higher.

Too bad they couldn't do anything about the Militia. The thugs had escaped. Every damn one of them. In the melee after their explosive vests were detonated, they'd retreated. Nobody was sure which way they went, only that they were gone.

Trevor came over to her bench. He slipped into a plaid wool shirt, leaving it unbuttoned, and sat beside her. He was close but not actually touching her. "Have you got a name for that puppy?"

"Not yet." She stroked the curly fur. "I can't keep him. Not with my work schedule. I don't want to get too attached."

"But he needs a name."

"Why?"

"A name defines who you are. You know that."

"I do?"

"Because your name is Sierra, you left Brooklyn and came west to the mountains." He looked down at the puppy. "Without a name, he doesn't exist."

"This sounds like a Cherokee thing."

"Could be," he admitted. "When I was born, my father stayed around long enough to name me."

"He called you Trevor?"

"No. A Cherokee name." He scratched behind the puppy's ears. "This poodle needs a brave name. Something that will make him ferocious."

"How about Rex?"

The puppy cocked his head and peered up at her with his black, shoe-button eyes. His pink tongue poked through his tiny sharp teeth, and he almost looked as if he was grinning.

"Rex," Trevor said. "King of all poodles."

Curious, she studied the man who sat beside her. "Are you going to tell me your Cherokee name?"

He shrugged. "It's not important."

"Come on," she teased. "Partners are supposed to tell each other everything."

"And we're still partners?"

"Of course," she said without a shred of doubt. "Now tell."

"My people come from the wolf clan, ancestors of the Cherokee war chiefs. My father must have known that I'd need the strength and cunning of my clan. Being half-Cherokee was sometimes hard and lonely. I had to be tough. So he named me Blue Wolf. Because of my eyes."

She saw a flicker of sadness in those eyes as he remembered his past. "Blue Wolf. I like it."

"So do I," he said.

In the soft glow of afternoon sunlight, his expression subtly changed. Though he remained serious, another emotion appeared. Concern? Determination? "What are you thinking about, Trevor?"

"Guess."

She leaned a bit closer. His eyes were a mystery. "I don't know."

"I'm thinking about you," he said.

A pleasant shiver went through her. That look in his eyes…was it desire? The fact that she didn't know for sure if he was into her meant she'd been out of the dating scene way too long. "In what way are you thinking about me?"

"Your bravery," he said. "And your stubbornness. If you hadn't been so mule-headed about rescuing the hostages, those people would have died."

Apparently his interest wasn't sexual. And she wished that it was. She wanted him to be thinking about her as a woman, viewing her with the same lust she'd been feeling for him. Didn't he want to make love to her? A few days ago, in her kitchen, he'd admitted as much. "Anything else?"

"Too much to put into words."

His gaze held hers. She could feel him leaning toward her. Their bodies drew closer. She could almost taste his lips. This was the moment when they should kiss.

Then he looked away. He leaned back against the wall of the barn and closed his eyes.

Well, fine! Don't kiss me. She mimicked his posture. They sat in silence. Side by side, not touching.

From the stalls, one of the horses nickered. There was an outdoorsy scent of hay and saddle leather. Her fingers tangled in the soft puppy fur. She should have been content rather than frustrated.

Softly, he said, "We were good as partners today."

"Damn good." At least they agreed about that.

"But I don't want you in danger. The Militia hates you. They'll come after you again."

"What else is new?"

"You should go somewhere else. I'll pay for your trip back to Brooklyn."

"Are you trying to get rid of me?" She sat up straight, and the puppy bounced in her lap.

"There's nothing more you can do here."

"Wrong."

"There's a statewide manhunt under way. The best trackers in the country are looking for—"

"That's like what you said today at the Galleria. Leave it to the professional lawmen? Hah! I was right to go after the hostages."

"This is different."

"I was right," she repeated. "The hotshot FBI negotiators didn't get it. But I did. I knew the Militia wouldn't keep guard on the hostages. I knew they'd kill those people."

"How did you know?"

She shuddered as an uncomfortable realization struck. When she was with Lyle, she'd lived in the presence of evil; she'd become familiar with it. "I hate to admit it, but maybe I understand these guys."

"Maybe you do."

His gaze sharpened, and she recognized his expression immediately. He wanted to use her, to probe around inside her head. "No way," she said. "If you're thinking about taking me back into your nasty little interrogation room, you can stop right now."

"Relax, partner." He grinned. "You can trust me."

Could she? When it came to physical protection, she totally believed in him. Trevor was a warrior first. Anything else he might feel for her came second. "You want to interrogate me, don't you?"

"There might be something in the back of your mind that could—"

"Forget it."

She rose from the bench and stomped through the open door of the barn into the late afternoon sunlight. The toes of her sneakers dug into the soft earth as she rounded the corral and stood at the edge of a rolling field of golden grass. The natural beauty failed to alleviate her confusion.

Trevor seemed to want her in a sexual way. But he also looked upon her as a source of information—someone to question and use. And then to throw away?

"Sierra? What's wrong?"

When he came up behind her, she whirled around. "I don't get it. I thought you were, you know, attracted to me."

"Hell, yes," he said.

"Then why are you trying to get rid of me?"

"Is that what you think?"

"Yeah."

His long arm encircled her waist, and he clenched her tight against his body. Before she knew what was happening, his mouth claimed hers with feverish passion. His kiss was so unbelievably hot that she melted like ice cream on a stovetop. Wonderful, delicious feelings oozed through her veins. Then her heart beat faster. A rush of pure sensation awakened every nerve, every muscle, every cell in her body. Though she had never kissed him before, except in a dream, this felt familiar and so very right.

When he loosened his grasp, she was dazed. All she wanted to do was make him happy. "You can ask anything you want, Trevor."

"What do you mean?"

He nuzzled her ear, and another starburst of sensation exploded.

"Interrogate me," she said.

"As you wish," he murmured. "Keep your eyes closed."

Already aroused, Trevor looked down at the woman he held loosely in his arms. This was going to be the most bizarre interrogation he'd ever done. There was no chance for his usual detachment. He cared too much about Sierra to think of her as a subject.

"Do it," she urged.

He took a moment to appreciate her copper-haired beauty. Her delicate features. Her lush body. She had more facets than a diamond. "Relax," he whispered. "Empty your mind of distractions. Breathe deeply."

When she inhaled, her breasts rose and fell, distracting him. He dragged his mind back to the interrogation. "Let your thoughts flow. Gently, like a slow-rolling river. Relax your body."

She followed his instructions, quickly sinking into an open state of mind. Because of their earlier interrogation, her subconscious was already attuned to the sound of his voice.

He continued, "I want you to remember the good times. Think back to when Lyle introduced you to the men in the Militia."

"I never liked Perry Johnson," she said. "He's a mean, vicious person. I told Lyle he shouldn't hang around with a guy like that."

"And what did Lyle say?"

"He was loyal to Perry and all the other guys. He thought Boone Fowler was some kind of god." She paused, thinking. "But I don't think Lyle completely trusted the Militia."

She frowned and gave a little wriggle. Damn, she was sexy.

"Did Lyle have secrets?" Trevor asked.

"There were things he told only to me. I liked that. It made me feel special."

She smiled, and the radiance that lit her face sparked jealousy in Trevor. He didn't want her to feel that way about another man, even if Lyle was dead. "What did he do to make you feel special? Did he bring you gifts?"

"Like a side of beef?"

She chuckled, again moving against him. Trevor didn't think he could hold her much longer without kissing those teasing lips. "Tell me."

"One time, we took off on a road trip. Just the two of us."

"Where did you go?"

"Two hundred or so miles. To this little town. I remember the name. Horton. Lyle said it was short for Whore Town. But I thought of something else." Her voice was slower than usual. Softer. "I remembered a book my mother used to read to me about an elephant named Horton. She's a nice woman, my mother. If she knew half the things that have happened to me out here in Montana, she'd be so upset."

Though he was curious about her family, he purposely derailed her memories of home and focused on the Militia and Lyle's secrets. "Tell me about the trip to Horton."

"We went into a bank and signed some papers." Her eyelids snapped open and she stiffened. "He opened a safe deposit box. Lyle was so proud, all puffed up. He promised he'd always take care of me and the ba—"

Her words stopped abruptly and she broke free from his embrace. Trevor knew what came next. The baby. The miscarriage. He hadn't intended to touch that memory.

"Interrogation over." Gently he placed his hand on her shoulder. "You did good, Sierra. There might be something important in that safe deposit box."

"I'm sure there is. Lyle told me that if anything happened to him, I should open the box."

"Do you have the key?"

She turned to face him. Her forehead had tightened in a frown. Raking up the memories of her past had squashed her passion. Sierra was no longer the willing, warm woman he had kissed a moment ago.

Trevor's interrogation had been successful on a tactical level. On a personal level, he was out of luck.

"I never had a key," she said. "Lyle kept that stuff, and I don't know what happened to it."

"All his personal effects were probably left at the Fortress prison. I'm not sure who was designated as his next of kin."

"It was me," she said. "I got a notification from

Warden Green, but I didn't bother to get Lyle's things. I didn't want to be reminded of him."

"So the key might still be there," Trevor concluded. "It's a thin piece of evidence, but worth the trip."

He wouldn't mind coming face-to-face with Warden Craig Green. His explanation of the Militia prison break had never made sense. Nor did the supposed suicide of Lyle Nelson. "Tomorrow we'll go there."

EARLY THE NEXT MORNING Sierra stopped at her duplex to change clothes and pack a couple of necessary items. Until the Militia was caught, she wouldn't be safe staying there all by herself.

Trevor insisted on checking out her house before stepping inside. There might be booby traps. While he inspected the door locks and peered through the windows, Sierra stood on the sidewalk and waited. In her arms, she held Rex, the ferocious poodle puppy.

When her neighbor came out, Rex gave a perky little yip. Sierra waved. "Good morning, Mrs. Hensley."

Instead of the usual snub, the gray-haired woman came nearer. She pointed with a long, skinny finger. "That's a dog."

"His name is Rex."

Tentatively, Mrs. Hensley took another step. Her pointed chin lifted, and she sniffed the air cautiously, as if Sierra might exude a poisonous odor. Another step. And another. This was as close as she'd come.

Sierra held the puppy toward her. "You can pet him. He likes to be scratched behind his ears."

As soon as the older woman touched Rex's soft, curly fur, her manner changed. No longer aloof, she murmured in baby talk.

Sierra handed the puppy to Mrs. Hensley. "It would really help me out if you could take care of Rex for a few days."

From the expression on the older woman's face, she might have just won the lottery. "I'll take good care of him. I had a puppy once. A poodle like this little guy."

"Thank you, ma'am. I really appreciate it."

"Take your time."

She pivoted and darted back into her house, moving very quickly for an elderly woman.

Trevor returned. "We're safe to go inside. Where's Rex?"

"I think he found a home."

In her bedroom Sierra changed and threw a few things into a suitcase. She might not be back here for a while. Obviously, she didn't have her job at the Galleria. And the coming of winter meant she wouldn't be working at the tree nursery, either. Unemployed in Montana. Was there anything so desolate?

But she wasn't sad. When she came into her front room and saw Trevor sitting on the sofa, his long legs stretched out in front of him, she almost felt good. Like Rex the ferocious poodle, she might have found the place she belonged. With Trevor.

THOUGH TREVOR WAS LOOKING forward to a conversation with Warden Craig Green, he hated the surroundings. The Montana penitentiary known as the Fortress was architecturally modeled after a medieval castle. If hell was cold and dank, this might be Satan's realm. As soon as he and Sierra stepped inside the heavy gates, he couldn't wait to get back outside.

The prison guards seemed to sense his discomfort. Instead of escorting them directly to the warden, they went the long way around.

"This here is cell block A," said a guard. "We keep the worst prisoners here."

The barred door at the end of the corridor clanged shut behind them. The cold stone walls of the prison seemed to close in. In his Special Forces training, Trevor had learned to endure all manner of discomfort, but the worst fate he could imagine was confinement. He stared straight ahead, avoiding the gazes of the men behind bars.

Sierra was farthest away from the cells, but the prisoners had noticed her. There were catcalls and lewd comments. Amid the other noise, a guttural growl reached Trevor's ears. *"Tsi-lu-gi, da-ni-ta, ga."*

He recognized the language. Those ironic words were spoken in Cherokee. *Welcome, brother.*

The man who had spoken pressed up against the bars of his cell. His hands dangled through the rails, and Trevor saw two crude prison tattoos. On the back of one hand was the seven-pointed Cherokee star—the same symbol Trevor wore on his silver ring. On the other was the outline of a howling wolf, the warrior clan. This prisoner could have been a distant relative.

Trevor stared into the hostile black eyes of the man behind bars. His frame was rawboned and huge. He wore his black hair long.

"Osi-yo da-ni-ta-ga wa-ya," Trevor said. *Hello, brother wolf.*

The fierce man did not smile. Nor did Trevor. In silent communication, they shared a moment of pain-filled recognition and sorrow.

"Hey," called the guards. "No talking. We gotta move along."

They left cell block A, and Trevor asked, "Who's the prisoner who spoke to me?"

"We call him Snake. He's half-crazy and all-mean. The most vicious son of a gun in the Fortress."

Trevor suspected that if he were imprisoned, he might have the same reputation. Inside these thick walls, all semblance of humanity disappeared.

In the warden's office, Trevor stood back and observed while Sierra did the talking. Warden Craig Green stayed behind his desk, emphasizing his position of authority. He adjusted his cuffs and nervously played with the knot on his striped necktie. Judging from his deeply lined forehead and the gray in his hair, the warden must be in his early sixties, Trevor guessed.

"Sorry for your loss," Warden Green said in a tone that lacked sincerity.

"Right," Sierra said. "I just want Lyle's personal effects."

"It's not much." He pointed toward a plastic bag that lay on his heavy oak desk. "Keys. A pocket-knife. A wallet. Less than twenty bucks in cash."

"Fine. I'll take it."

As Trevor glanced around the office, he noticed that the heavy bookcases were mostly empty. There were bare spaces on the walls where pictures might have hung. "Looks like you're moving."

"Time for me to retire," Green said. "I've given twenty-two years to this place."

The timing was suspicious. Only a few months ago Boone Fowler and the Militia had staged a successful escape from this formerly impregnable prison. "After such a long career, it's a shame you have to leave in disgrace."

"What the hell are you talking about?"

"The suicide of Lyle Nelson."

"We did all we could for that poor bastard." He nodded to Sierra. "No offense, miss."

"None taken."

"And the prison break," Trevor probed.

Green's eyes narrowed. "That was investigated. Not my fault."

"But it was never completely explained. The actual escape route was never determined."

"Things happen in prison that nobody on the outside can understand. That escape was one of them."

Green's shoulders were tense. One hand clenched on his belly, causing Trevor to wonder if he had an ulcer. "Is that why you decided to retire? The unexplained things that happen here?"

"None of your business." The warden sat behind his desk. "Take your things and leave."

"When's your last day?" Trevor asked.

"The new warden arrives on Tuesday next week. After that, I'm history."

And all his secrets would vanish with him. Trevor sensed he would see the warden again. And their next meeting would be even less cordial.

Chapter Ten

Dressed in camouflage, Perry Johnson hunkered down beside a granite outcropping in the forested lands surrounding the Fortress penitentiary. Even from half a mile away, he could smell the stink of prison. There was no need to get close. Only one highway led to hell.

Unlike some of the other men, especially Lyle, Perry had used the years he'd spent incarcerated as a test of his endurance. When it was cold in the Fortress, he'd stripped off his shirt and drawn the chill into his bones. When it was dark, he'd kept his eyes closed so he'd be blind. Every minute of every day, he'd exercised, flexing and extending until his muscles were harder than the stone walls that imprisoned him.

When they escaped, Perry had been tougher, stronger and meaner than when he went inside. Confinement in hell had honed his rage sharper than the eight-inch serrated blade he always carried at his side.

Motionless as a granite statue, he stared at the stone turrets of the prison. The rest of the Militia were back at their hideout, celebrating their assault on the Galleria. But Perry had other scores to settle. Sierra Collins had to die.

Earlier today, he had spotted her at the dumpy little duplex she'd once shared with his buddy, Lyle. She was with a tall cowboy. From the way she looked at him, Perry could tell that she was sweet on this guy. That little witch! How could she betray Lyle's memory with a half-breed? When he saw what was going on, Perry was tempted to raise his rifle, aim and shoot them both.

But he was a patient man. He would wait for the exact right moment. A time when there would be no witnesses. A time when he was sure he could escape.

Strategy was important, and Perry was one of the best damn hunters in the state of Montana or anywhere else. Stalking his prey took careful restraint, and it would be worth his time. When he slaughtered Sierra, he'd do it up close. He wanted to see the terror in her eyes, to hear her whimpers of pain when he plunged the knife into her gut and twisted.

He shifted his weight and scowled at the Fortress. What the hell were they doing inside?

Using his cell phone, Perry called Boone. "They're at the Fortress."

"Keep following," Boone instructed.

"I could take them when they head back to town. It would be easy to disable their vehicle and—"

"Not yet."

"Why not? There's a good three miles of deserted road. I could shoot out the tires, kill them and be on my way before anybody noticed."

"Not yet," Boone repeated. "That's an order."

Without another word, Perry disconnected the call. He could wait. Soon, very soon, he would take his revenge on Sierra and her boyfriend. Maybe he ought to scalp that half-breed.

WHEN TREVOR PARKED outside the bounty hunters' headquarters, Sierra experienced none of her former hesitation about going inside. She'd spent last night in the guest room here. She'd slept late, had a leisurely brunch and gone for a horseback ride with Trevor. The headquarters felt almost like home. Still, she asked, "Why do we need to come here? I've got Lyle's keys, including the one to the safe deposit box. We should go directly to the bank in Horton."

"I want to check in," Trevor said. "Don't worry. We'll make it to Horton."

"How?" She glanced at her cheap wristwatch, which tended to gain time. "It's already after two, and this is a long drive. Four or five hours. We'll never get there before the bank closes."

A sexy grin lifted the corner of his mouth. "How do you feel about helicopters?"

"You're joking."

"Hey, partner. You know me better than that."

Yes, she did. Trevor wasn't a man who wasted time with cornball jokes. When he said he was going to do something, it usually happened.

"A helicopter?" Zipping to Horton on a chopper seemed like an alien concept in this land of horses, cowboys and rugged outdoors. But she was definitely up for the ride. "I've never been in one before. But, wow! I'd love it."

Being with Trevor was one unexpected adventure after another. As they walked toward the porch, a giddy excitement churned inside her. Ever since he'd ridden into her life on his dappled mustang stallion, things were different. Definitely better. He had pulled her out of a humdrum life of boring jobs and lonely nights. They had a mission, a purpose. It was fun to be on the side of the good guys.

Inside the headquarters, the mood was less cheerful. At a table near the dartboard, the handsome Riley Watson conversed quietly with Joseph Brown, the tracker who apparently had a crush on Princess Veronika of Lukinburg. He'd crossed paths with Prince Nikolai's beautiful younger sister a few times during the course of their investigation in to the Militia escape. The other men teased him unmercifully about his royal "girlfriend."

Tony Lombardi from the Bronx, and Mike Clark, who was quiet and smart, frowned at the wide-screen television, where a news commentator was discussing the ramifications of the terrorist attack on the Galleria.

Tony gave her a nod. "Hey, Brooklyn. How are you doing?"

"Not bad for somebody who just got back from the Fortress."

"Did you find what you were looking for?"

"You bet."

"Any word on Murphy?" Trevor asked.

"He's stable," Mike Clark said quietly. "Off the respirator but still in the hospital. The docs don't know how badly the exposure to potassium cyanide will affect him. It could screw up his vision."

"Damn," Trevor muttered.

His broad shoulders tightened, and she could feel the tension and sadness radiating from him. She glanced around the room. All these men were wound tight. Cameron Murphy was more than their former commanding officer. He was their leader, their hero, the man they looked up to.

"Mia is keeping us posted," Tony said.

Sierra hadn't met Cameron's wife, Mia, or his four-year-old daughter, Olivia. Apparently, the bounty hunters' headquarters was usually a female-free zone.

"Where's Powell?" Trevor asked. "We want to use the chopper."

"Not today." Riley Watson left the table and saun-tered up beside them. "Powell is working with the feds on aerial surveillance. They're looking for signs of the Militia. After they made their escape from the Galleria, they disappeared like phantoms. Vanished."

"There's nothing to track," Tony said.

"Nothing at all," Joseph echoed.

A frustrated silence fell over the room, and Sierra pressed her lips together, holding back her inappropriate excitement about riding in a helicopter and chasing the bad guys. It was going to take more than a grin and a chuckle to cut through this morose mood.

On the television, a panel of experts discussed the worldwide war on terrorism, comparing the Militia assault in Montana with ongoing terrorist activity in the Middle East, Russia and Lukinburg.

On the TV, a heavyset man in a dark suit said, "Though the Galleria assault was not part of a larger plot, there are similarities. The despicable targeting of innocent victims. The sophisticated weaponry. The insistence upon making a statement."

"Are you suggesting a link?" the commentator asked. "Do you believe the Montana Militia is a terrorist cell?"

"Not at all. But their techniques are—"

"They need to be stopped." A uniformed general with a chestful of ribbons weighed in to the discussion. "All terrorism. Everywhere. It needs to be stopped."

"Prince Nikolai Petrov of Lukinburg has requested aid from the United Nations and the United States."

"And he will get it," the general said.

"A preemptive strike?"

The general lowered his voice. "If the decision was up to me, I'd use an assault team. Skilled and highly trained."

Tony talked back to the television screen. "You said it, General. Send in the Special Forces."

"Damn straight." Joseph Brown strode toward the television. "Send us. We're ready."

"I know why you want to go to Lukinburg," Tony teased. "To impress Princess Veronika."

"That's got nothing to do with the way I feel about terrorists." Joseph scowled. "I can't even think about that sweet gentle lady at the same time I'm—"

"Quiet!" Riley snapped. He pointed to the television screen. "The general is sending a message. I'll bet there's already an operation under way. Special Forces is going in."

Just as he got their attention, the news program concluded, and a commercial about laundry detergent flashed across the wide-screen TV.

Riley turned toward them. "Mark my words, gentlemen. A skilled and highly trained military team is going to Lukinburg to eliminate the terrorist threat."

"It ought to be us," Joseph said with a quiet vehemence that was more intense than a shout.

The barely suppressed rage of the bounty hunters simmered, at the edge of a boil. The temperature in the room seemed to rise by several degrees. In the stone fireplace, the burning logs snapped and crackled. Sierra drew closer to Trevor, instinctively seeking shelter.

Mike hit the mute button on the remote before he turned toward them. "Gentlemen, we need to take it down a notch. We're no longer in Special Forces. We're bounty hunters."

"Once a soldier," Joseph said, "always a soldier."

"He's right," Tony exclaimed. "This is about a whole lot more than nabbing a bounty. People died at the Galleria. Innocent people. And Murphy's in the hospital. We won't let the terrorists win."

"We need to keep emotion out of this," Mike said. "We can't afford to be less vigilant, especially now that the Militia know who we are."

"I hope they come after us," Joseph muttered.

Trevor stepped forward. His voice was calm and controlled. "In the meantime, Sierra and I have a clue to track down."

"What's that?" Riley asked.

"Lyle Nelson's safe deposit box."

"What's in there?"

"Don't know," Trevor said. "But he went to a lot of trouble to keep the location a secret. There might be something in that box that could lead to the Militia."

"Stay in touch," Mike said.

"I've got my cell phone."

Trevor took Sierra's arm and led her from the room. As soon as she stepped outside, she took a deep breath. The brilliant afternoon sunshine and the clean, fresh air were a relief. She murmured, "I'm glad the bounty hunters are the good guys, because you're a bunch of scary dudes."

"Highly skilled and trained," Trevor stated. "Just like the general said on TV."

"Have you done that kind of stuff before? Sneaking into a country on a special mission?"

"Only when it was necessary. A well-trained platoon is more effective than a regiment."

"Like I said. Scary dudes."

AT THE MILITIA HIDEOUT, Boone Fowler listened with half attention as his men told and retold the story of their exploits at the Galleria. The bomb explosion. The taking of hostages. The final escape.

The men were happy. As far as they were concerned, their assault was the stuff of legend.

Unfortunately, Boone could not wholeheartedly join in their self-congratulations. The burden of leadership lay too heavily on his shoulders. He was concerned about the Puppetmaster.

The prearranged time for the Puppetmaster's call was near. Boone stared at his cellular phone, which was rigged to bounce the signal from satellite to satellite in an untraceable pattern. He was unsure of what to expect.

On some counts, he expected a reprimand. The Puppetmaster had wanted a death count in the hundreds. But the explosion rigged in the food court hadn't been powerful enough to knock down the support beam. And the hostages had escaped unharmed. Damn Sierra! That was her fault. From an insider account, Boone had heard that she and that half-breed bounty hunter had managed to spring the hostages in the nick of time before the potassium cyanide was released.

And now they were up to something else. According to Perry, she'd taken off on some other wild-goose chase.

His phone rang.

He went to the far end of the bunkhouse and answered, "Yes?"

"You failed, Boone." The voice of the Puppetmaster was harsh and furious. "I ordered disaster and chaos. An attack worthy of the Militia."

"Your purpose was served," Boone said, forcing himself to be confident. "I've been listening to the news. All those fancy-pants pundits are woofing and wailing about how we need to crack down on terrorism and—"

"You promised me death on a grand and horrifying scale. Instead, I have newspaper photos of policemen rescuing puppies from the Galleria pet shop."

The tension in Boone's gut tightened into a painful knot. "We discovered the identity of the men who have been thwarting our actions. Cameron Murphy, their leader, is in the hospital."

"The bounty hunters," said the Puppetmaster.

"Formerly of U.S. Special Forces. Their involvement interests me."

He sounded somewhat appeased, and Boone tried to build on that tenuous thread of approval. "We could attack them. They could be our next target."

"Don't even think about it," the voice sneered. "You and your pathetic band of misfits don't make a move until I say. Remember that, Boone. Not one move."

Static crackled through the cell phone, and Boone listened hard. His very survival depended on the Puppetmaster. Without his financing, the Militia would be dead and their cause—their sacred cause— forgotten forever.

"Never fail me again," the Puppetmaster said. "Or your fate will be far worse than a trip back to prison."

"Give us another chance," Boone said quickly.

"You'll have your opportunity. There will be another assignment very soon."

The phone connection went dead. When Boone clicked the off button, he realized that his palm was slick with nervous sweat.

He quickly punched in the cell phone number for Perry Johnson, who was tailing Sierra. As much as they all wanted to see her dead, that wouldn't happen now. Not until the Puppetmaster gave the order.

Perry answered, "What?"

"Don't kill her," Boone said.

"Why not? She's a thorn in our side. And her half-breed boyfriend is one of the bounty hunters."

Which might be useful. The Puppetmaster had been interested in that connection. And Boone wanted to strike at those guys. He wanted to hurt Cameron Murphy. To hurt him bad.

Though Boone had been instructed not to make plans until further notice, he thought the Puppetmaster would approve of this action. "Take them hostage," Boone said. "See if they have information that would be useful to us."

"Hostages?"

"Keep them alive," he warned.

"I will," Perry said. "But by the time I'm done with them, they'll wish they were dead."

"CAN I DRIVE?" Sierra asked.

"No."

She leaned back in the passenger seat of Trevor's Jeep. They'd been on the road for almost three hours and were now winding along a two-lane road bordered by pine forest on one side and a steep dropoff on the other. The ascent to the top of this mountain pass seemed endless, but she was in no rush. Through the windshield, she watched the last glimmers of sunlight fade into a gentle, gray dusk.

"I love this time of day," she said. "It's so peaceful. There's a park in Brooklyn where I used to go and watch the sunsets."

"On the East River," he said.

"Have you been there?"

"No."

Then how did he know what she was talking about? "Did I mention this place before?"

He nodded. Trevor had a habit of reading her mind, and she figured it wasn't just skill. She'd told him things in that interrogation room—personal things. "That park on the East River," she said. "It's beautiful."

"A special place," he agreed.

Her mind flashed back to a hazy moment when she'd been relaxed and dreaming about her special sunsets, and Trevor's voice had poured over her like warm brandy. The wisp of memory faded, and Sierra shrugged, not wanting to dwell on the ugliness of their first meeting. She liked Trevor now, liked him a lot. More than anything, she wanted to trust him.

"In New York," she said, "dusk brings an incredible transformation, as the skyscrapers light up. But out here, it's a miracle. When night falls, the dark comes really fast and then a million stars fill the skies. I can't believe how many! At night, when I look up, it's like I'm inside one of those glass balls filled with glitter."

The lights from the dashboard shone on his strong profile, and she saw him grin. "What are you thinking?" she asked.

"I was imagining you as a little girl, turning a glitter ball upside down. I bet you were a cute kid."

"No way. I was a pain in the butt. You might have noticed that I'm kind of mouthy."

His grin spread wider. Though Trevor wasn't big on talking, he was a good listener. The way he paid attention made her feel as if she was witty and clever—worthy of his interest. Again, she asked, "Can I drive?"

"No."

"Come on, Trevor. I'm a really good driver, and you've got to be tired by now."

"I'm fine," he said. "We're less than an hour away from Horton."

They had already called ahead and found out that the bank was open from nine to noon. Tomorrow, they'd go there and search Lyle's safe deposit box. But tonight was an open question. They hadn't discussed what they'd do for sleeping arrangements. After that kiss yesterday, she had some very sexy ideas.

"When we get down from this pass, we should start looking for someplace to stay." Like a motel with a soft double bed where two people would fit nicely in each other's arms.

"We could camp," he said. "I always carry a tent and sleeping bags in the back."

"Aren't you the Boy Scout? Always prepared."

"When I'm on the trail of a bounty, I don't want to waste time looking for a motel."

But he wasn't actually bounty hunting right now. It was just the two of them. And she didn't care for the idea of making love for the first time on the hard forest ground with no shower.

Thinking that she might have to throw his tent out the back window, she glanced toward the rear of the Jeep, where his gear was neatly arranged. "What else have you got packed away in there?"

"Tools of the trade."

"The bounty hunter trade," she said. "Guns?"

"A rifle with a nightscope. Listening devices. Binoculars."

"I'm surprised you don't have one of those global map thingys in the car."

"I had one but took it out. I didn't like the idea of someone being able to track my vehicle." He nodded toward the glove compartment. "I have a handheld GPS locator that I can turn on. In case I need to let the other guys know my location."

Night descended quickly. The soft light of the rising moon shone through the windshield and illuminated his features. She recognized his Cherokee heritage in his high cheekbones and strong nose.

As she studied him, a little tremor of excitement shot through her. She couldn't help but admire his virility. Any woman would recognize that Trevor was a desirable man, but she was beginning to see deeper than his thick black hair and his wide shoulders. Inside, he was even more handsome. Honorable and brave. In a way, heroic. All the bounty hunters had that aura.

"You guys are more than friends," she said. "More than bounty hunter business associates."

"We're brothers."

"You'd do anything for them, right?"

"Right."

"And how do you feel about partners?" she asked. "Like me? Do you think of me as a sister?"

He cast a sidelong glance in her direction. "Not hardly."

She knew he was attracted to her; his kiss had proved that. But Trevor was hard to read. His interrogator training had taught him how to hide his emotions. She wanted to know how he really felt about her. Was he looking for a quick roll in the hay? Or something more? "When you look at me, what do you see?"

"Your dark eyes," he said, "shining with life force and energy. Then I see your wild hair, curling like spun gold. And then there's your body. Your amazing body."

"It's not so great," she said. "I don't look like a model or anything."

"You look like a woman. Strong and soft at the same time. When you bend over in your tight jeans, it's something to behold."

"Oh, yeah." She gave a self-deprecating chuckle. "My butt is definitely one of the wonders of the world."

"And don't get me started talking about your lips. Your full, lush, beautiful mouth." His Adam's apple bobbed as he swallowed. "Lips that are meant to be devoured."

Wow! When this quiet man put his thoughts into words, he was pretty darn fluent. "I guess it's safe to say you don't think of me as a sister."

"I wouldn't be a man if I didn't admire the way you look," he said. "But don't get me wrong. We're partners, too. I owe you my loyalty, and I'd protect you with my life."

For once, she didn't have a smart-aleck comment on the tip of her tongue. His sincere commitment to her as a partner was overwhelming. And his appreciation of her as a woman was somewhat daunting. Trevor was a lot to take after five years without a man. She almost wished she'd had a couple of practice dates with guys she didn't care about before meeting him. All these little quivers she felt inside were building into a full-blown earthquake inside her. Was she ready? Did she dare give her heart once more?

Needing to lighten the mood, she asked again, "Can I drive?"

"No."

"Is there some logical reason why not? You can't possibly think there's any danger. We haven't seen another car in ages."

"All right. I'm tired of arguing the point. You can drive."

He pulled onto the shoulder and parked. Quickly, she leaped from the passenger seat and scampered around the hood. Halfway, she met Trevor. Face-to-face in the headlights, they stood for a moment. A breeze swirled the crisp night air around them, and she could hear rustlings from the forest.

She looked up at him, then her gaze lifted to the night skies, where pinpricks of stars glimmered like an array of diamonds. It was their night. The stars belonged to them. Tentatively, she lifted her hand and placed her palm flat against his chest. His body radiated warmth. Strength. Maleness.

She felt him surrounding her, pulling her closer. Then his head whipped around as though he'd heard something.

"What is it?" she asked.

His eyes narrowed as he peered through the moonlit forest behind the Jeep. "Something's out there."

"Probably a deer," she said. "Do you see it?"

"I feel it. A presence."

She patted his chest. "Nice try, Trevor. But there's nothing there, and I'm still driving."

Quickly, she circled the car and got behind the steering wheel. After adjusting the seat and the mirrors, she fastened her seat belt and eased back onto the winding, two-lane mountain road.

"I like the way your Jeep handles," she said. "It's got a lot more power than my little car."

"Four-wheel drive," he said. "If you go into a skid, you're supposed to—"

"I know how to drive," she said impatiently. People

in Montana made a big deal about how hard it was to drive in the mountains, but she'd learned to dodge cabs on the streets of Manhattan and racing along the Long Island Expressway. Her reaction time was top-notch.

They crested the mountain, still surrounded by trees. Though it felt as if they'd been climbing for hours, the elevation was below timberline. Still, she noticed that the drop on the open side of the hairpin turns was steep.

Trevor turned in the passenger seat and stared through the back window at the road behind them. "There," he said. "Somebody's following us."

She glanced in the rearview mirror. "I don't see headlights."

"His lights are off."

That couldn't be a good sign. No sane person would drive mountain roads at night without headlights.

Trevor flipped open the glove compartment and took out a handgun. "Drive fast, Sierra."

Chapter Eleven

Trevor never should have let her drive. Spending these unguarded hours with Sierra had lulled him into a sense of complacency. He hadn't been expecting an attack, hadn't been thinking about the Militia and how much they hated the woman who hunched over the steering wheel, concentrating on the narrow mountain road. Though she was doing a good job of negotiating these twists and hairpin turns, he wished that he was the one in the driver's seat.

There was nothing he could do about his position. Not now.

For the moment, he figured they had an advantage. The driver of the car creeping along the road behind them didn't know he'd been spotted. These moments could be used to speed ahead.

Trevor checked his handgun. He had a full clip, but if it came to a shootout, he wanted a rifle for accuracy and distance. And his rifle was in the back.

Unfastening his seat belt, he edged between the bucket seats.

"What are you doing?" Sierra asked.

"Keep driving. We need to put distance between us and that other car."

The tires squealed as she zipped around a sharp turn, but he didn't complain. The logical strategy was to get off these treacherous mountain roads and onto relatively flat, open highway where they could make a run for it. From behind the back seat, he grabbed his rifle and a box of shells. He peered through the rear window and saw the glint of moonlight on the other car. It was coming closer.

The headlights flashed on.

Quickly, Trevor returned to the front seat with his rifle.

Beside him, Sierra gripped the steering wheel with white-knuckled fists. Her brow lowered as she peered into the night.

"You're doing fine," he assured her.

"Have you got a plan?"

"Keep driving." His fear was that the car behind them would link bumpers and force them off the road. If Trevor had been in pursuit, that was what he'd do. "We want to reach flat terrain."

Her eyes flicked toward the rearview mirror, and she cringed. "He's getting closer."

"You're okay. Concentrate on the road."

"I am."

She swooped through a series of curves. The distance between them and the car following grew wider. Impressed, he said, "You really are a good driver."

"Mountains are easy," she said. "You should try getting through Chinatown on a Saturday night when you're a teenager and late for curfew."

Trevor rolled down the passenger side window. They were on a relatively straight stretch of road. He leaned out, trying to aim at the tires of the car behind them.

But the driver of the other car was quicker. A shot rang out. Then another.

The left rear tire of Trevor's Jeep exploded. They fishtailed as they approached another bend in the road.

Sierra hit the brakes and barely made the curve, overcompensating to avoid the steep dropoff. The Jeep careened toward the sheer rock wall on the opposite side. She pulled back in time, but they had lost significant speed.

It was vital to disable the other vehicle.

From the passenger side window, Trevor fired at the tires of their pursuer and hit the target. The headlights were perilously close.

The other car jolted and slowed. Success!

The driver responded with another volley of bullets. The right rear tire of the Jeep went flat.

Sierra kept going, as fast as she could. "Trevor! We're almost down. We're coming out of the trees."

At the edge of the road, he saw the glint of a mountain stream. If they were on foot, an escape through the forest would be safer than on the open range where they had no cover. "Slow down," he said.

"No way!"

"We have a better chance if we're out of the car."

The vehicle behind them whacked their bumper, and the Jeep jolted like a bucking bronco. Sierra fought the wheel and brought them safely around another curve. "Where do I stop?"

"Pick a wide spot." He reached inside the glove compartment and took out the GPS device, which he turned on and slipped into his pocket. Then he grabbed his cell phone and punched in the number for headquarters.

"What are you doing?" she panted.

"Calling for backup." As soon as someone picked up, he spoke into the phone. "This is Blackhaw. We're being pursued. I have my GPS locator on. Get here fast."

The car behind them smacked the rear of the Jeep again. The sickening crunch of metal echoed loudly. The air bags popped open. Sierra was blinded, and the car careened wildly.

With one arm, Trevor fought the bag in front of her. He heard the screech as she stomped hard on the brakes, and he yanked the steering wheel tight to the left. They went into a spin.

Unable to see, he imagined them twirling off the

edge of the road. Instinctively, he grabbed Sierra's arm, pulling her toward him, trying to protect her, to shield her against...

The crash! The impact jolted him with bone-wrenching force. He couldn't tell what they'd run into, what they'd hit. They were at a dead stop.

Frantically, he pulled the air bags out of the way. "Sierra, are you okay?"

"Been better," she gasped.

"Are you injured?"

"I don't think so." There was no sign of fear in her expression, but she was dazed. In shock. "Trevor, tell me what to do."

In the Galleria, when they'd taken on the Militia, he'd been impressed with her reactions. She was a good partner.

He spoke clearly. "Unfasten your seat belt. You're coming out the passenger side door behind me."

As she struggled with the air bag and the belt, he reassured her. "We're going to make it."

"What makes you so certain?"

"We're the good guys, Sierra." He knew it was a glib and meaningless solace, but he wanted to boost her confidence. "The good guys never lose."

"What do we do next?"

"I'll go first. As soon as I'm out of the car, I'll start shooting." The best defense was a strong offense. He might get lucky and nail the son of a bitch who'd destroyed his Jeep. "You run for the trees."

"And you?"

"I'll catch up with you. Don't stop running," he ordered. "Don't look back."

He shoved open his door and emerged, gun first. Trevor made a quick dive and roll. He had only ten rounds in his bolt-action sniper rifle, which was designed more for accuracy than for laying down a barrage of firepower. Every shot needed to count.

Moonlight reflected off the other vehicle. It was about twenty yards away. Though less damaged than Trevor's Jeep, steam rose from under the hood.

From behind the Jeep, Trevor took his shots.

Return fire came from behind the other car. The driver was staying with his vehicle. It was good to know where he was.

Trevor heard Sierra exiting.

"Go!" he ordered. "Into the trees. Run and stay low."

"How will you find me?"

"Follow the stream. Downhill."

She leaned against his back, and he felt the weight of her body—her sweet, beautiful body. If anything happened to her, he'd never forgive himself. "Go!"

As she started toward the trees, he stepped out from behind the Jeep, making himself a target. He fired three times.

Their pursuer fired back. A bullet pinged against the metal, inches away from Trevor's left shoulder. This guy was a damn good marksman.

Trevor returned fire. Only five rounds left in the rifle.

He scooped a rock off the road and flung it up the hillside, where it landed with a crash. He hoped to distract the marksman, but didn't really think such a simple ruse would work. He'd bet this guy was a hunter.

But if he'd meant to kill them, he would have shot through the windows of the car instead of disabling the tires. Trevor feared there was some other agenda at work.

After releasing another shot, he took off after Sierra. He dived into the forest and leaped down the embankment. In just a few strides, he was at the stream. The rippling water shimmered in the night like a silver ribbon. Sierra wasn't far ahead of him. On the opposite side of the creek, she stopped and turned toward him.

Trevor had been in firefights more times than he could count. Never before had he felt this quiver inside his chest. It was fear. For the first time in his life, he was scared. Not for himself. But for her.

Charging heedlessly across slippery rocks, he reached her side and grasped her arm. He was breathing hard, gasping, fighting the panic that rose up within him and threatened to blank his mind.

"We're going to make it," she whispered.

"Damn right." He shook his head, clearing the cobwebs. The warrior in him emerged. No time for fear. She was his woman, and he would protect her. No matter what.

In a glance, he surveyed the terrain. He changed course. They needed to get to higher ground so they could see their pursuer. Across a clearing, the land rolled higher. But he didn't want to chance being targeted in the moonlight.

If they went back to the road, they might find a safe ridge. And their pursuer wouldn't expect them to double back. Trevor pointed. "This way."

She offered no objection as he linked his hand with hers and tugged. He stayed in the trees as they backtracked. They were making too much noise, but there wasn't time to creep silently. Sierra stumbled, and he hauled her upright.

They crossed the road and went higher, dodging between tree trunks, until they found a good vantage point. He pulled her down beside him. They stretched out flat, peering over the edge.

In the darkness, the only movement came from the wind shaking the branches of conifers.

"Do you see him?" she whispered.

Trevor shook his head and held his finger to his lips, signaling silence. Carefully, he scanned the rugged, forested hillside. On the worn two-lane road, he could see his Jeep. The major impact of the crash had been to the hood, which was crumpled. There would be no driving away from this collision.

Trevor closed his eyes and listened. He was usually able to sense the presence of another person. But not this time. All he heard was the whisper of the forest. Either they had outsmarted their pursuer and he was still trudging along the stream, or the marksman who was after them was an experienced hunter, soundless in the forest.

When Trevor opened his eyes again, he was surprised. The other vehicle was limping slowly along the road below them. The engine rattled, and the rim of the exploded tire scraped on the pavement. The driver stopped directly below them but did not get out of his car. In a harsh voice, loud enough for them to hear, he snarled, "This isn't over, Sierra. I'll keep coming after you. Night and day. You'll never know when I'm going to strike next."

His vehicle moved away.

"Perry Johnson." Her voice trembled. "He's always hated me, even when I was with Lyle."

"Why?"

"Perry thinks women should be submissive. You know, cooking and cleaning. House slaves. That's not my style."

"Is he a hunter?"

She nodded. "A legendary hunter and fisherman. Unlike a lot of survivalists, he's got the skill to back up his commitment."

Then why hadn't he come after them? If Perry's goal was to kill Sierra, he was in the right place to stalk them. It seemed even more ominous that he'd been willing to leave. The Militia was up to something. Again.

AFTER FIVE MILES of hiking through the forest, Sierra thought the Piney Lodge Motel looked as luxurious as The Plaza on Central Park. Though there were no liveried doormen, no marble entryway and definitely no chandelier, the inside of the square little room they rented was warm. And there was a queen-size bed. Arms open wide, she flung herself across the flowered bedspread.

All kinds of intense thoughts and emotions had swirled through her during their long trek, which had to be more than five miles no matter what Trevor said. While she'd been moving, concentrating all her efforts on putting one soggy foot in front of the other, it had been easier to control herself. Now those emotions penetrated her flesh and sank deep into her heart. The fear she'd held at bay consumed her. Perry Johnson had promised to kill her, and he wasn't the kind of man who gave up. She knew he'd keep coming. Night and day, he'd pursue her until he had his revenge.

If it had been Boone Fowler or any of the other Militia, she wouldn't have been so scared. But she'd looked into the cold black eyes of Perry Johnson. She'd seen him up to his elbows in blood when he'd skinned that deer. She imagined herself as that helpless animal, hanging by her heels as Perry ripped out her liver and carved her body into steaks. He was a force of nature, purely evil and highly skilled. He enjoyed the stalking and the ultimate kill.

Trevor flopped onto the bed beside her. He'd been busy on his cell phone. Tomorrow morning the bounty hunters would meet them here at the Piney Lodge Motel. The GPS gave their precise location. His colleagues who were expert trackers could start from here to follow Perry Johnson. "Bloodhounds," he said.

She turned her head to look at him. "Is this a game? Am I supposed to name another dog? Poodles?"

"I just got off the phone with Tony Lombardi. They're going to use bloodhounds to track Perry Johnson."

"And this is good news?"

"It is for us," he said. "There are more than the bounty hunters involved in this manhunt. The feds and local sheriff are in on the chase. Perry Johnson has gone from being the hunter to being the prey. He's going to be too busy protecting his rear to worry about us."

But Trevor didn't know Perry. He wouldn't be deterred, couldn't be stopped. "He's mean as a rattlesnake," she said. "I wouldn't be surprised if he crawled into his hole for the night and came out ready to attack us."

"For tonight, we're safe."

She wanted to believe him. Sierra was too tired to even think about another chase. Still, she wasn't totally convinced that they were safe. Tension played at the edge of her consciousness like a bad tune that was stuck in her head. "Just in case, I'd feel a lot better if you slept with your gun under your pillow."

"I'll be ready." He lightly stroked her cheek. "I'll take good care of you."

The sincerity in his voice touched a chord within her, and she knew that he meant what he said. "Trevor, are you ever afraid?"

"Only a fool feels no fear."

"You're always so confident. The whole time in the Galleria. And when we were being chased down the mountain and shot at. You always know exactly what to do."

A shadow crossed his face. "Tonight, I was scared to my bones. Just for a minute, I was shaken, unable to breathe. I never felt like that before."

"Never?"

"I've been well-trained. I know how to handle attack and pursuit. I know the defensive moves. Under fire, my brain is working too fast, coming up with the next logical strategy, that I don't have time for emotion. But tonight was different."

"How so?"

"Tonight, I was with you."

In spite of her fear and exhaustion, she began to warm from the inside. Her heart fluttered a bit faster. "Go on," she whispered.

"I knew that if you were harmed, my life would be worthless. You're all I dream about. If you were taken from me, it would be worse than death."

"That's beautiful."

"It's the truth."

She knew he wasn't lying. Trevor wasn't the kind of man who spoke falsely. He was true and brave and so very sexy. The gleam from his blue eyes hinted that he wanted to kiss her senseless.

She was all he dreamed about. Her instincts told her that making love to him would be fantastic. Why not? They were alone in a motel room, lying side by side on a queen-size bed. Why the hell not?

Because she was scared. She'd thought she was in love with Lyle. And that had resulted in five years of misery. It was safer to be alone, fighting her own battles. And yet some things were worth taking a risk for. Trevor was worth it.

He patted her shoulder and sat upright. "You need to have a shower and warm up before you get under the covers."

"Join me," she said. The words popped out before she had truly considered them.

He gazed down upon her. "What are asking me to do?"

More firmly, she said, "Join me in the shower."

Chapter Twelve

Trevor didn't need a second invitation. Now that Sierra had taken the first step—no matter how hesitant—he wasn't about to let her turn back.

He knelt beside the bed and loosened the laces on her sneakers, which were still wet from their escape through the mountain stream. Gently, he removed her shoes and socks. Even her well-shaped feet were sexy. He rubbed the soles. "You're ice-cold."

"Not for long," she said.

He stood and took her hand. With a light tug, he pulled her off the bed and into his arms, where she landed with an awkward thud. She was tense; he could see it in the set of her jaw, could feel it in her tight muscles, could hear her nervousness as she exhaled a ragged breath.

Though he was anxious to strip off her clothes, drag her into the shower and make love to her, Trevor knew this was a time for patience. He glided his hands up her arms to rest on her shoulders. "Are you scared right now?"

"Should I be?"

"It's been a long time for you," he said. "For me, too."

"That's hard to believe." She tilted back her head so she could look him in the eye. "I mean, Trevor, you're gorgeous. You must have women throwing themselves at you."

"Not at all."

"I bet you and the other bounty hunter hunks have more babes than you can handle."

"Lombardi is a ladies' man. So's Watson." And their exploits were mythic. "But not me. I'm picky."

Cautiously, he leaned forward and kissed her forehead, then the tip of her nose.

She jerked backward, intending to move away from him. But he held her in place. *Not this time, Sierra.* This time, she wasn't going to run away from her feelings. Or from him.

She tossed her head, sending a ripple through her thick, golden hair. "Why pick me?"

He traced the line of her full lips with his index finger. "The first words I heard from this pretty mouth were after you spat on Lyle's coffin. You told him to burn in hell."

"That turned you on?"

"It told me that you're a woman of deep passion— a brave woman who doesn't care what other people think. You're a challenge, Sierra. A woman worth waiting for."

And his time for waiting was over. His lips claimed hers in a long, hard kiss. He tightened his embrace, pulling her luscious body against his chest. Tonight, she would be his.

As he kissed her again, he felt her resistance wane. The tension in her muscles relaxed as her arms encircled him. She swayed against him. The rhythm of her heartbeat synchronized with his. The dance had begun.

His hips moved against hers, and she responded gracefully. *Follow my lead, Sierra.* Her back made a subtle arch. Her full, beautiful breasts pushed against him, and he could feel her tight, hard nipples. When he cupped her sweet flesh, she gave a little cry that became a soft moan of pleasure.

With gentle insistence, he unbuttoned the waistband on her denim jeans and slid the zipper down. Her skin was delicate, smooth and tantalizing. He wanted to tear off all her clothes. Instead, he maintained taut control, carefully unlocking the treasures of her body, proceeding at her pace.

Her jeans were gone. Her shoes were off.

When he started to slide the fabric of her T-shirt over her head, she stopped him. She stepped back.

He swallowed hard. If she called a halt right now, he was pretty damn sure that he'd erupt like Mount Saint Helens. His erection throbbed. His need for her was all-consuming.

She took another step away from him. "I'm going to the shower now. Join me in a few minutes."

When the bathroom door closed behind her, he sank onto the bed. His whole body was one big erogenous zone. He'd never been so turned on. How much longer should he wait? A few minutes? Literally? Should he count to sixty twice?

The hell with that! He peeled off his boots and his clothes and tossed them aside. Before he charged into the motel bathroom, he remembered: protection. From his wallet, he took out a packaged condom. And he grabbed his handgun.

Through the bathroom door, he heard the sound of the shower. He twisted the knob and stepped inside. Wisps of steam circled the tiny white-tiled bathroom. The shower was a bathtub with frosted glass doors that showed a pink silhouette of her voluptuous body. *Let me in there!* He tucked the gun under her discarded T-shirt.

Sierra slid the shower door open and peeked out. Her brazen gaze surveyed his naked body. "What are you waiting for? An engraved invite?"

"I'm ready."

She glanced down at his erection. "I see."

When she looked up to his face and grinned, he felt a surge of happiness. He was almost giddy. "Let me see *you.*"

"Like this?" She pushed the frosted glass door aside and stood before him, naked.

Water droplets clung to her satin skin. Her full breasts were perfect globes. Her small waist flared out into rounded hips. "Aren't you the prettiest thing I've ever seen."

"Am I?"

"Oh, yeah."

He was in the shower with her. His hands slathered soap across her body, as hers did to him. Then they rinsed with special care until they were both sleek and hot and clean. She turned her back to him, and he washed her thick hair, twisting the strands between his fingers. The falling water slid down her spine and over the perfect round swell of her buttocks. She was incredible. He turned her around to lick the spray from the crook of her neck and to nuzzle her breasts.

When she touched his erection, he shuddered. "Don't."

"But I want to."

"I'm hanging on by a thread, Sierra. I don't want this to be over too soon."

"Don't worry," she teased. "We can always do it again. And again."

He sheathed himself with the condom, then yanked her close. Her slick body glided against his as she wrapped her arms around his neck. With the water from the shower pelting his back, he pressed her against the shower wall, nudging her legs apart with his knee. Holding her firmly, he entered her. She closed around him, hot and tight.

Their groans of pleasure echoed against the tile. Gasping wildly, she rocked against him.

The pressure was more intense than he'd ever felt before. He couldn't wait one second more.

"Now," she cried. "Now. Now."

Gratefully, he took his sweet, earthshaking release. For a moment, the world stood still. Gravity was gone. He felt as though he'd passed out and gone straight to heaven. It was the finest lovemaking he'd ever experienced.

He looked down at Sierra. Her head lolled back against the tile wall as she exhaled a shivering sigh. Her eyelids opened slowly. Through her thick lashes, she gazed at him with an expression he had never seen before.

He couldn't wait to do this again.

THE NEXT MORNING, Sierra thought the sun might be shining a little more brightly. The air might taste more pure and fresh. Last night, when she and Trevor made love, her world had changed, and this was definitely a better, more hopeful place to live.

At half past nine, Mike Clark picked them up at the Piney Lodge Motel. Sierra was glad Mike was driving. The intelligence expert that Trevor referred to as the "human lie detector" was much more discreet than Tony from the Bronx, who would surely have teased them about spending the night together. Such jokes wouldn't have been appreciated. She didn't want to talk about their lovemaking; it was still too new and special.

She sat in the back seat of the SUV behind Mike and Trevor, listening as the two men discussed the ongoing search for Perry Johnson. The car he had been driving was located, but provided no clues because it was stolen. Then Perry had swiped another vehicle. Then he'd been on foot, on the run from an army of law enforcement officials and bloodhounds. Still he'd escaped.

She should have been scared, but fear was far from her mind. She couldn't take her eyes off Trevor. Swept away by a tidal wave of infatuation that would have been corny if it hadn't been so real, Sierra knew she was glowing. Her cheeks were warm. Her mouth wouldn't stop grinning. She showed all the classic symptoms of a woman who had been well-loved the night before. Once in the shower. Twice in the bed. And then they'd run out of condoms, which was fortunate because they could have gone on all night and she would have been too sore to walk, too blissful to think, too satisfied to do anything but lie on her back and sigh.

When Trevor turned in his seat and looked back at her, his blue eyes smoldered. His lips curved in a proud, possessive smile. He should have been speaking words of passion. Instead, he asked, "Do you have the key for Lyle's safe deposit box?"

She dug into her pocket and pulled out her ex-fiancé's key chain. "Right here."

"If the bank gives you a problem about opening the box, we can get a court order," Trevor said. "But we might as well give it a try."

She nodded. That wasn't all she'd like to try with him. They were definitely buying more condoms today.

Mike parked on the main street of the small mountain town. The Horton bank was on a corner, distinguished from the other storefronts by a stone facade. "This is the place," she said.

When she'd come here with Lyle, they might have even parked in this exact spot. The memory of that day wasn't unpleasant. They'd talked about her pregnancy, and Lyle had promised he would always care for her and his child. Hah! What a liar.

She slammed the car door a little harder than necessary and fell into step beside Trevor—a man who always told the truth and meant what he said.

Inside the bank, Sierra automatically reverted to her former identity as an administrative assistant for a Wall Street law firm. Her tone was assertive and businesslike when she presented the safe deposit box key and identified herself to a self-important young man in a black suit. Even though she was dressed in jeans, a T-shirt and parka, the young man responded to her attitude.

He checked his records and nodded. "Ms. Collins, you're listed as a co-owner of the box."

"Am I?"

"That's right." He handed over the forms so she

could read them. Lyle had filled out one. And her signature was on the bottom of the other.

Vaguely, she remembered filling in her name, but she hadn't attached much importance to this stop at the bank in Horton. When Lyle brought her here, she'd been more focused on the fun she'd been having on the road. Maybe this box was important, after all.

She signed a ledger book, and they followed the bank clerk down a flight of stairs to a lower level, where he retrieved the metal box from a vault and led them to a small private room. After Sierra thanked him, he closed the door and left them alone.

She sat at the square wood table with the box in front of her. "What do you think is in there?"

"I'm hoping it's a map to the Militia's hideout," Trevor said. "What's your guess?"

"Why would Lyle need a safe deposit box? After Boone took all his money, Lyle didn't own anything of value. Not like jewelry or coins or anything. When we got engaged, the ring he gave me cost less than fifty bucks."

She plugged the key into the box and opened it. Inside was a manila envelope and a spiral notebook. From the envelope, she removed a stack of documents and scanned them quickly. Her background in legal matters came in handy as she deciphered the meaning.

"It's a life insurance policy. I'm the beneficiary."

This was a big fat surprise. She had never expected Lyle to do anything as practical as planning for the future in case something happened to him. A life insurance policy? Amazing!

"It's probably lapsed by now," Trevor said.

She checked the figures and the dates. The policy was all paid up through the end of next year, and the cost of the premium had been substantial. At first glance, it looked as if the policy had been purchased before Lyle hooked up with Boone, back in the days when good old Lyle actually had a family fortune. Then, five years ago, he'd changed the beneficiary to her.

She flipped through the pages and read the numbers. She blinked, rubbed her eyes and read them again. "The payout is one million dollars."

Trevor gave a long, low whistle. "He never told you about this policy?"

"Never."

Sierra stared down at the papers, the letters and numbers blurring as her eyes filled with tears. Lyle Nelson had been a mean son of a bitch who'd slapped her, shoved her and stolen her savings. As a member of the Militia, he was responsible for mass murder and terrorism. A terrible person, he was a villain of the first order.

And yet he had cared about her and their unborn son. This document was clear evidence that in some deeply buried part of his soul, he'd tried to do the right thing.

Trevor placed his hand on her shoulder, and she held on to him, drawing comfort from his touch.

"Lyle wasn't all bad," she said. "I grew to hate him so much that I forgot about the good times."

"This must make you happy," he said.

Startled, she looked up at him. "Why would you say that?"

"Now you finally have enough money to leave Montana. You can go back to Brooklyn and restart your life."

"With this money? It doesn't seem right."

"You're the beneficiary. The money is yours."

Confused, she shook her head. "Lyle was Militia. He did terrible things. If I profit from his death, it seems like I'd be linked with him forever."

"Are you saying that you're not going to cash in the policy?"

"Of course I will." She dashed away her tears and looked up at him. "I might have ethics, but I'm not a fool. This appears to be a legitimate document."

"It's a lot of money."

For a moment, she was tempted to take the money and run. She pushed back her chair from the table and paced in a tight circle. A million dollars. It would take her a lifetime to save that much.

Her brain revved on all cylinders. She could buy a house. A new car. She could go to college.

She pivoted and paced counterclockwise. If she and Trevor had a million dollars, they could go anywhere and do anything. She wouldn't have to work two part-time jobs just to make ends meet. And Trevor could quit being a bounty hunter and risking his life...not that he'd want to quit. His work wasn't about the paycheck.

And her life wasn't about cashing in on misery, sorrow and pain. Yes, she'd had some good days with Lyle. But that didn't change who he was—a member of the Militia who had been responsible for the deaths of innocent people. A terrorist.

Taking money from that source could only bring pain. Her ticket to a better life would have to be purchased with something other than this cash.

Integrity didn't come cheap.

Bye, bye, million dollars.

"I made up my mind," she said, still pacing furiously. "I'll take the payout and donate every penny to the fund set up for the families of the Galleria victims."

"Good decision." Trevor stepped into her path and gathered her into his arms. "You're doing the right thing."

Reaching up, she took off his hat and tossed it on the table beside the insurance policy. Her fingers stroked his smooth black hair. "I think I deserve a kiss."

"A million dollar kiss?"

"Do your best."

He snuggled her body against his, awakening memories of last night's passion. He was so tall that it seemed impossible they'd fit together, but they did. Her breasts grazed his broad masculine chest. Their legs entwined, and his erection rubbed against her thigh.

His mouth teased her lips apart. His tongue darted. Then he deepened the kiss. Instinctively, he knew exactly where to touch her body. He knew when to stroke, when to squeeze and when to caress softly as a whisper. All her senses were aroused.

"Nice," she murmured.

"Very nice," he echoed.

She wrinkled her nose. "But I think that kiss was only worth about two hundred thousand."

"Don't worry, partner. I'll pay the rest tonight."

"Even if it means making love until dawn?"

"It's for a good cause."

Though he stepped away from her, she could still feel his embrace. He was a part of her. All she wanted was to be with him, to stay in his arms and let the rest of the world take care of itself for a while.

He picked up the spiral notebook that was on the table. "What's this?"

"A journal." With a sigh, she dragged herself back to reality. "I gave it to Lyle so he could write down his thoughts."

"You make it sound like he'd write poetry."

"The closest Lyle ever got to poetic was singing country-and-western ballads off-key. I wanted him to journal as a way of focusing. He had trouble expressing himself. Like most men."

But not Trevor. When he chose to speak, he was nearly eloquent.

She took the spiral notebook from his hands and randomly flipped open to a page that listed all the things Lyle needed to buy at the grocery store. "This wasn't why I got him a journal. He was supposed to write down his innermost thoughts."

But Lyle had never been a deep thinker. On another page, he had scribbled a primitive sketch of a horse. Most of the entries were brief accounts of what he'd done for the day. "Trip to hardware store." "Ate burger and fries at café." "Went hunting with Perry Johnson."

She shuddered. Even this childish journal brought back the very real danger Lyle had caused her. Hunting with Perry? Less than a day ago, Perry had been hunting her.

Farther back in the notebook were several ominous references to the Fortress prison. "He mentions Warden Green by name. In here, he says that Green has the answers."

"That might be something we should look into," Trevor said.

A return trip to that dank, cold penitentiary wasn't her idea of a fun outing. "Why?"

"We have another reason to talk with Green," Trevor said. "I'm sure that million dollar policy has a clause that invalidates the payout if the death was a suicide."

"You're right. That's standard procedure." And Lyle's death had been ruled a suicide. "I never believed that he killed himself. Lyle was too stubborn and mean to take his own life. But can we prove he was murdered?"

"We can try," he said.

"It would be a shame to deny this million dollar payoff for the families of Galleria victims."

"Right." Trevor looked away from her. "I've been wanting to have another conversation with the warden before his retirement."

The determined tone in Trevor's voice worried her. Another meeting with Warden Green, especially if they were questioning the circumstances of Lyle's death, was sure to be trouble.

Chapter Thirteen

Late afternoon at the Militia hideout, Boone glanced up as Perry Johnson crashed through the door. The big man looked as if he'd been in a landslide. His clothes were torn. Fresh blood from a deep scratch oozed across his forehead. His coal-black eyes flared with demonic light. He snarled, "Damn you, Boone. What was so all-fired important that I had to get back here right away?"

As leader of the Militia, Boone couldn't allow disrespect. Though Perry was a powerful presence, Boone had to be stronger. He stood slowly, shoulders back. His mouth curved in a sneer. "Sit down, Perry."

"Tell me what's going down. Tell me now."

"Sit!"

Growling, the other man obeyed. "I almost had them. Sierra and her half-breed boyfriend." His huge hands grasped empty air. "I could have taken them both hostage. I could have—"

"You didn't stand a chance," Boone said. "We

were monitoring the police radios. They knew your location and were already closing in."

"It wouldn't have taken long."

"I can't afford to lose you, Perry. Not now. We have another mission. Something big. Am I right, men?"

They nodded enthusiastically; their excitement was palpable. Raymond edged closer to Perry and held out a glass of water. "You're going to like this, Perry. It's big."

Somewhat placated, Perry grabbed the water and downed it in one gulp. "I'm listening."

"A military base," Boone said. "We will strike at the heart of the oppressors. We will demoralize the government."

Amid murmurs of agreement from the men, Perry spoke up. "Where is this base?"

"Back east."

"I don't like to leave Montana," he grumbled.

"We have to go where the battle lies," Boone said. "We have to take the fight to them."

The logistics of this assault were more complex than anything the Militia had undertaken, but Boone was confident. After their well-coordinated Galleria attack, he knew his men were capable.

The Puppetmaster would handle transport and provide weapons. The Militia would take care of the rest.

"Our assault on the Galleria was effective," Boone said. "Those fat-ass bureaucrats in Washington sat up and took notice. They fear us. They want to strike back. But they can't find us."

"So we attack them first," Raymond said. "Before they know what hit them."

"Who?" Perry demanded. "Who do we attack?"

"Special Forces," Boone said.

According to inside information from the Puppetmaster, the U.S. government was finally ready to act on behalf of Prince Nikolai of Lukinberg. Nikolai wanted troops to take action against the terrorists in his homeland, and the U.S. agreed. They were about to deploy a Special Forces platoon on a surgical strike.

As a bonus, this Special Forces platoon belonged to the same unit that Cameron Murphy had formerly commanded. They were his comrades and the heirs to his reputation. Attacking them would be a devastating blow to Murphy and his bounty hunters.

Frankly, Boone was glad they'd be leaving Montana. From his constant monitoring of law enforcement communications, he knew the manhunt was coming closer. If the Militia stayed here, the danger of being discovered was imminent.

"One question," Perry said. "What happens to Sierra and the half-breed?"

"Warden Green will take care of them."

"Green? I thought he'd retired."

"Not yet," Boone said.

Less than fifteen minutes ago, he'd given the order

to Warden Green: kill Sierra and her boyfriend. The sniveling warden objected, saying he'd already taken too many risks. But he'd changed his mind when Boone had informed him that if he didn't follow this order, he would be the next target for the Militia's revenge.

WARDEN CRAIG GREEN RESTED his elbows on his desktop and silently cursed Boone Fowler and the Militia. Damn them for demanding one more job, one more risk. It wasn't fair. Green was only hours away from his retirement. He had cleaned out his office, had already arranged for a charter plane to fly him to Denver, where he'd catch a flight to Costa Rica. The money paid to him by the Puppetmaster for arranging the Militia escape had already been transferred to an untraceable offshore bank account. That sum was more than enough for him to live in luxury for the rest of his life.

He should have been celebrating. He'd gotten away with everything—the Militia escape and the murder of Lyle Nelson. But now he had one more job.

Killing Sierra Collins and her boyfriend wouldn't be easy. There was sure to be an intense investigation—especially from those damn interfering bounty hunters.

He needed a plan to cover up these murders until he was safely out of the country. Somehow, he had to make sure their bodies would never be found.

SIERRA PRESSED CLOSE to Trevor as they were escorted by a prison guard through the dank corridors of the Fortress penitentiary. They'd been searched; anything that might be used as a weapon had been taken from them, and she felt particularly vulnerable amid all these armed guards and desperate prisoners.

In each sector, barred doors were unlocked for them to pass through. As the heavy doors slammed shut behind them, the harsh metallic clank echoed against the stone walls. A chill seeped through her parka and her T-shirt. She had a real bad feeling about this meeting with the warden.

Trevor had told her that he suspected Warden Green of being involved in the Militia escape and in the supposed suicide of Lyle Nelson. But Green wasn't about to confess, especially not now when he was on the brink of retirement. Still, Trevor thought the warden might be convinced to point the finger of blame at someone else.

When she'd asked how he was going to do that, Trevor had given her a quick lesson in interrogation techniques. "The carrot and the stick," he said. "We promise him a reward. Then we threaten punishment."

His system had sounded too simple when he explained it. Now, the idea seemed flimsy as tissue paper. They were walking, unarmed, into a lion's den.

Warden Green rose from behind his desk to greet them. Though the desk, chairs and equipment were still in his office, all his personal property had been packed away.

"Looks like you're ready to go," she said.

"It's my last day." When he shook her hand, his palm was clammy. "What can I do for you, Sierra?"

"We had a few questions," she said. "About Lyle's death."

"You're welcome to look over the reports." He also shook hands with Trevor. "The investigation was pretty much open-and-shut. Lyle couldn't stand the thought of being back in prison, and he killed himself."

"Is it possible," she asked, "that someone might have helped him along?"

"Murder?" The warden gave a hollow laugh. "Not likely. He was locked in a cell all by himself. There were guards watching."

"They couldn't have been watching too closely if he managed to kill himself."

"These things happen." Green returned to his desk and sat, looking contented as a toad. "The guards were reprimanded and suspended for a week without pay."

She perched at the edge of a straight-back wooden chair on the opposite side of the desk, unable to think of anything that might cause Green to change his story.

Apparently, Trevor had an idea. Instead of sitting, he stood with his arms folded across his chest. "There's a reason we're interested. A million dollar reason."

The warden's brown eyes flickered with sudden interest. "A million dollars?"

"Lyle Nelson had a life insurance policy, all paid up until the end of this year. Sierra is the sole beneficiary."

"Interesting." Green leaned his elbows on his desk. "I suppose the policy is invalid in case of suicide."

"If you were inclined to reopen the investigation and change the cause of death, we'd be grateful. Say, two hundred thousand in gratitude."

This was the carrot. Sierra had to admire the way Trevor dangled it before the warden's nose.

"Is that a bribe?" the man asked.

"A reward," Trevor amended

"Even if I were inclined to accept a bribe, that figure sounds low. Unless Lyle's death is ruled a murder, you'll get nothing."

"How much?" Trevor asked.

Green cleared his throat and nervously tugged at the knot on his necktie. "Seven hundred thousand seems fair."

As Trevor bargained with him, the warden stepped deeper into the snare. The figure they ended up with was half a million.

Quickly, Green added, "Not that I'm saying I could be bought. That wouldn't be legal."

"Unless Lyle's death really was murder," Trevor said. "Then you'd be telling the truth. Righting a wrong."

The warden nodded in agreement. "Yes, I would."

"This prison is filled with killers. Any one of them might have gotten into that cell with Lyle."

Green's tongue darted across his lips as though he could already taste this newfound fortune. "If I opened an investigation right now, the new warden would have to deal with it."

"And he might find Lyle's killer." Trevor's voice held an encouraging note. "There's no risk to you. And a big payoff. Half a million dollars would make a tidy nest egg for your well-deserved retirement."

The warden was practically drooling. He wiped the back of his hand across his mouth. Sierra knew this man could be bought. His ethics and his years of service as warden were no match for his greed. What other terrible things had he done for payoffs?

"There's another issue to discuss." Trevor's voice had changed from cajoling to accusing. "We found Lyle's journal. You're mentioned several times."

"All lies," he said. "Lyle was a vindictive bastard. He showed no respect."

"I want your side of the story," Trevor stated.

Green backed off. "I don't know what you're talking about."

"The Militia. Worthless scum, all of them."

"You're right about that."

"Killers."

"Yes."

"They threatened you." Trevor's eyes narrowed. "They're still threatening you."

The warden shuddered. He looked scared.

Trevor circled the desk and turned Green's

swivel chair so they were face-to-face. Leaning close, Trevor continued his intimidation. "The Militia is vindictive. You said so yourself. They need to be caught and put away where they can't hurt you."

For a long moment, the warden stared into Trevor's eyes. "I'll help you catch them. For half a million dollars."

Though it appeared that Trevor had won, he showed no sign of triumph. As he stepped away from the warden, he seemed almost reluctant to continue.

She sensed that something in his interrogation had gone wrong. When Trevor had been peering into Green's eyes, he must have seen something that disturbed him.

"I can show you how they escaped," Green said eagerly.

An alarm screeched inside her head. Why would Green show them the escape route? Surely, that would implicate him. She glanced up at Trevor. "I don't think we need to know how they got out."

"Suit yourself," Green said. "But I'm leaving town tonight on a charter plane, and I'm not coming back. The secret of the Militia escape leaves with me."

She could tell that Trevor was curious. "Show us."

Green rose from behind his desk. "We'll need a guard to accompany us. Say nothing about what we talked about in here."

In the corridor outside Green's office, Trevor took

her hand and squeezed lightly. He leaned close and whispered, "He's not going to hurt us."

"How can you be sure?"

"Green is too much of a coward. He knows he'd be caught."

The warden motioned to them. "Come along. I'm taking you to an area that few people outside the Fortress have seen. We call it the dungeon, appropriate for this castle."

Certain that they were being led into danger, Sierra tightened her grasp on Trevor's hand. Her feet felt like they were weighted with lead; she didn't want to take another step.

The guard unlocked a heavy wooden door and shoved it open. When they went through, he locked it again and followed them.

They descended a short stone staircase. The ceiling in the dungeon was low, less than eight feet high. There were no windows. The only illumination came from two bare lightbulbs.

Green led them to a wall of four cells. Inside one of the cells was the inmate Trevor had spoken to on their previous visit to the Fortress, the Cherokee they called Snake.

Trevor paused outside the bars and nodded to him, showing respect. "We meet again, brother."

"Don't talk to him," Green warned. "He'd just as soon kill you as look at you. Mean as a snake."

Trevor spoke a few words in a language she didn't

understand. The other man responded by touching the tattoo of the seven-pointed Cherokee star on his forearm, then he turned away.

"Snake spends a lot of time down here," the warden said. "The dungeon provides perfect isolation. You could yell or scream for hours, and nobody would hear you."

"Why are we here?" Sierra asked.

"There's something you need to see." He motioned them toward the last cell in the row.

From her peripheral vision, she glimpsed motion behind her back where the guard had been standing. She heard the impact of a blow. With a groan, Trevor collapsed on the floor.

Sierra whipped around and saw the guard. He dropped the billy club he'd used to knock Trevor unconscious, and came toward her. Before she could think, before she could react, he'd cuffed her hands in front of her.

Then he turned to Green and said, "That's all I'm doing. I ain't killing nobody, Warden. No matter how much you pay me."

"Of course not," Green said smoothly.

"I'm not proud of the stuff I've done for you."

Frantically, Sierra appealed to the guard. "You won't get away with this. People know we're here."

Green scoffed. "Your bodies will never be found. By the time anybody figures out that you're dead, I'll be long gone."

"What about me?" the guard asked. "I'm not retiring."

"I'll take care of you."

The barred door to Snake's cell crashed open. He leaped on the guard. In one swift, brutal movement, he snapped the guard's neck.

Frozen in fear, Sierra stood rooted to the stone floor. Inside her head, she heard a high-pitched scream. Her life was over. And Trevor's. They would die together before they'd even had a chance to live.

"It's a shame to kill you," Green said as he sauntered to the farthest cell in the dungeon. "I was tempted by your offer. But if I admitted that Lyle's death was murder, I would be implicated."

She stammered, "Y-you killed him?"

"Lyle was threatening me, and I had him taken care of." He nodded toward Snake. "Much the same way I'm going to take care of you and your boyfriend."

At the farthest cell, he yanked hard on one of the bars. It came off in his hand.

"Crowbar," he said. "Snake, give me a hand. Bring her into this cell."

The huge man roughly grabbed Sierra's arm and shoved her toward the bars. Her legs were stiff; she could hardly move. There was no chance of escape from this place. If she screamed, no one would hear her.

Green counted off paces and indicated the place on the floor where Snake should use the crowbar. It took a mighty effort, but one of the flagstones lifted.

"And this," said the warden, "is how the Militia escaped."

He had freed them. Warden Green had turned those animals loose on the world, and they had killed again at the Galleria. Anger cut through her fear. There had to be something she could do; she didn't want to give up without a fight.

"This," he said, "is where your bodies will be hidden."

Sierra knew they wouldn't be found. After the Militia escape, the prison had been thoroughly searched by law enforcement. None of the experts had located this escape route.

The warden gave his final instructions to Snake. "Kill them both and put them into the hole. Put the guard in there, too. Your reward is freedom. This hole leads into a mine shaft. From there, it's open country."

The big man lifted his chin and smiled.

"He's using you," Sierra said vehemently. "Don't you see? He's going to blame everything on you."

"He's already a prisoner," Green said. "I'm giving him a break."

Walking away quickly, he ascended the staircase leading out of the dungeon. At the door, he looked back over his shoulder. "Goodbye, Snake."

The heavy wooden door closed behind him.

Sierra stared into the black eyes of the big man. "What's your name?" she asked. "Your Cherokee name?"

"Deer Hunter," he rumbled.

She tried to remember everything Trevor had told her about the beliefs of his tribe. "Listen to me, Deer Hunter. If you harm me, or Trevor, whose Cherokee name is Blue Wolf, you will never find peace. In the afterlife, we'll be ghosts and we'll find you."

He hauled the body of the guard to the hole in the floor and shoved him through.

"Please," she continued desperately. "Please, Deer Hunter. You've got to help us."

He lifted Trevor under the arms and dragged him across the floor toward the hole.

Sierra couldn't stand by and watch while Trevor's neck was broken. "No," she shouted. "You can't kill him."

She leaped toward the big, dark man. With her cuffed hands, she battered his arm.

He gave her a shove, knocking her to the floor. "I will have my freedom."

And that was all that mattered to him. There was no way she could fight this man.

Sierra scrambled across the stones. She was on her knees beside Trevor's unconscious body. Her cuffed hands rested upon his chest, above his heart. Leaning down, she kissed his lips for the last time.

He gave a groan and stirred. Life was so cruel. He was returning to consciousness in time to feel the pain of dying.

"Sleep, my darling," she said softly. "I love you."

These might be the last words she uttered in this lifetime. Though she and Trevor had shared only a brief moment of happiness, she had that joy to carry her into the next world. If there was any justice, they would be reunited.

In this reality, there was no chance of escape.

Chapter Fourteen

Deer Hunter grasped her shoulder and wrenched her away from Trevor's unconscious body. He pointed to the hole in the floor. "You go first."

Holding her cuffed wrists in front of her face for protection, Sierra staggered back against the stone wall of the dungeon cell.

"Go," he snarled.

She shook her head. "I'm not going to make it any easier for you to kill me."

"I won't kill you, woman. Not unless you wish to die."

Unsure that she'd heard him correctly, she lowered her hands. In the dim light, she peered into the scarred face of this violent man. He was someone to be feared. Moments ago, she'd seen him murder the prison guard. "You won't hurt me?"

He pointed to Trevor. "Your man is a warrior. Cherokee like me. To take his life would dishonor our fathers."

She believed him. Deer Hunter had no reason to waste his breath in lying to her. He wasn't going to kill them. "What should I do?"

"Go in the hole."

Sierra obeyed, lowering herself into the shallow space. Once there, her head was even with the stone floor of the dungeon. The hardpacked earth beneath her feet slanted sharply. When she gave a nudge to the dead guard sprawled beside her, he rolled down to a deeper level, where she could barely see him in the thick darkness. Green had said this was a mine shaft that led to freedom, but she couldn't see the escape route.

Reaching up with her cuffed hands, she helped Deer Hunter lower Trevor into the cave. Gently, they carried her fallen warrior to the lower level, where the floor was flat.

Deer Hunter returned to the opening above them. With an impressive exertion of strength, he lifted the flagstone and covered the hole.

Absolute darkness surrounded her, and she clung to Trevor's jacket. He was beginning to wake up. His arm moved, and he groaned.

She heard Deer Hunter slide down beside her. In a low rumble, he said, "I will leave you now. Blue Wolf will care for you."

"Thank you," she said. "Thank you, Deer Hunter."

"My freedom is thanks enough."

She heard him moving away, but couldn't tell

which direction he was going. Never in her life had she imagined a place could be so dark.

She crawled across the cold dirt floor, fumbling until she found the body of the prison guard. Not allowing herself to think about the fact that she was touching a dead man, she searched his pockets until she found the key to her handcuffs and freed herself.

So far, so good. She was making progress.

In the dark, she heard Trevor draw a shaky breath. "Sierra."

"I'm here." She scooted toward the sound of his voice. "I'm right here."

"I can't see."

When she touched him, he fumbled until he held her. His hands were shaking. "Are we dead?"

"Not yet, partner."

The profound darkness enclosed them like a shroud.

WITH GREAT SATISFACTION, Boone Fowler listened to the phone call from Warden Green. Sierra and her half-breed were dead.

The timing was perfect. Boone had received confirmation on their next mission—an attack at the heart of the corrupt government that sought to destroy the real freedoms of the people. In only a few more minutes, a helicopter would land outside their hideout and take them from Montana.

There was one more task Boone needed to handle

before their departure. He placed a call to the Big Sky Bounty Hunter headquarters.

When someone answered, he said, "Tell Cameron Murphy that his Special Forces unit will be attacked and destroyed as a lesson to him. The deaths of those men are on his head."

With a click of his thumb, he ended the call.

Boone expected the bounty hunters to react to this challenge. With no thought for their own safety, they'd stupidly make plans to rescue and protect their comrades-in-arms. It was their credo: never leave a man behind.

All the while, Boone would have the upper hand. He was calling the shots.

Life didn't get much better than this.

IN THE CAVE, enclosed by stifling darkness, Trevor faced the terror of his worst nightmare—being confined. He was sightless. Trapped. With no escape.

Where was he? How did he get here? His heart pounded so hard it felt as if it might burst. *Can't think. Can't see. Can't breathe.*

"There's a way out of here," Sierra said. "Trevor, do you hear me?"

He couldn't show her his fear. Didn't want her to panic. "What happened?"

"Long story." Her voice quavered. "We're in a mine shaft under the dungeon. This is how the Militia escaped. You were right about Warden Green. He helped the Militia, and he arranged for Lyle to be murdered."

Though he knew she was telling him important information, only one word penetrated Trevor's dread, and that was *escape*. "How do we get out of here?"

"Don't know." Her fingers touched his face. "How's your head? You got whacked pretty hard."

He was too overwhelmed to feel the pain. If given the choice, he'd take a knife in the gut instead of this dark confinement. But nobody had given him an option. He was here, trapped in this hellhole. He had to deal with it.

Disoriented, he thrust one arm straight out. He groped. There was nothing but empty air. He couldn't tell right from left, up from down, couldn't even see his own hand. They'd never escape. They would run out of air. His lungs ached from breathing so hard.

"This way," he muttered. By sheer force of habit, he took control, inching across the floor until he felt a wall. His fingers clawed at the dirt. The wall was unstable, apt to disintegrate and crumble. They'd be buried alive. *I can't do this. I can't move.*

Feeling hopeless, he leaned back against the wall. The pressure of his panic tightened around his throat like a noose. He couldn't breathe. "Sierra, I want you to go on without me."

"Are you nuts?" Her snippy voice cut through the thick darkness. "I go nowhere without you."

"Just leave."

"Yeah, sure. I'm going to abandon the sexiest man on the planet." She grabbed his shoulders and shook him hard. "You owe me eight hundred thousand in kisses, and I intend to collect."

Though it seemed impossible, the terror loosened its grasp upon him. He took a breath and filled his lungs. This was better, much better.

His hand was drawn to her waist. She felt solid, real, strong. His fingers crept up her rib cage. His despair waned as he cupped the fullness of her breast. "If I can find this in the dark, I guess I'll be okay."

"Too bad it doesn't light up."

"Come closer, Sierra."

He embraced her and drew strength from her resilience, her stubbornness, her affection. As long as she was with him, Trevor knew he could survive. For her sake.

"Cell phone," he said.

"Nice thought. But I don't think you're going to get a signal down here."

He dug into his pocket and pulled out his phone. When he flipped it open, the faint green light shone like a beacon.

"Much better," she said.

"Just great." Now he could see how narrow the tunnel was. The walls began to close in once more. "Have I ever mentioned that I'm a little bit claustrophobic?"

"We'll talk about it later," she said.

With his back against the wall, he pushed himself

to a standing position. "Do you have any idea which way to go?"

"Not a clue."

"You hold the phone," he said.

With one hand on the wall and his other arm wrapped tightly around her, he moved forward a step, then another and another. "The floor slants upward."

"So?"

"A mine shaft would be drilled down. So the entrance has to be uphill. As long as we keep going up, we're headed out."

They made good progress until they came to a fork in the tunnel.

Sierra held the phone for better light, then she pointed. "That way is up."

"Got it." But he hated to let go of the wall. Without that anchor, it felt as if he would drown in the inky darkness. Taking a breath, he plunged forward until his fingers touched another wall.

They followed the tunnel around a sharp turn. The floor kept rising. There was another fork.

"This place is a labyrinth," she said. "I think we're going in circles."

"We're closer to the exit." He could feel it. The air had changed. The faintest whisper of a breeze touched his cheek. "Almost there."

And yet they kept stumbling through the endless passageway. It felt as if they'd been there for days.

His throat was parched. The back of his head where he'd been clubbed was beginning to ache.

"Stand still," she said.

Without asking why, he did as she asked. From behind them, he heard the crunch of a footstep on gravel. They were not alone in the tunnel.

When he looked over his shoulder, Trevor saw nothing. The illumination from the phone didn't shine far enough. "Let's get the hell out of here."

Another twist, another fork. He listened for another sound behind them but heard nothing. The person following them was stealthy.

Around one more sharp angle, they stepped into a wider space that was familiar to Trevor. He'd been here before, on a search with the bounty hunters. This cave—the interior of an abandoned copper mine—was a hideout the Militia had used after they escaped from the Fortress.

More importantly, Trevor saw the way out—a gray glimmer. He moved quickly toward it. Heavy boards covered the exit, but he was so anxious to escape that he tore through them.

He stepped outside. The gush of fresh air intoxicated his senses. He was free.

"We made it!" Sierra shouted.

He yanked her into his arms and twirled her around. In the fading light of day, he peered into her dancing eyes. "If it hadn't been for you, I never would have gotten out of there."

"You need me." She grinned impishly. "I like that."

He kissed her like there was no tomorrow. When their lips parted, he whispered, "We need to find a bedroom. Fast."

She nodded and handed him the cell phone. "Call your buddies for a pickup."

Trevor glanced back at the gaping mouth of the abandoned mine shaft. He'd been careless. Before kissing Sierra, he should have made sure they weren't being followed. Yet he saw no sign of pursuit.

As they followed a sloping path toward a stream, he put through a call to bounty hunter headquarters.

Clark answered and snapped with uncharacteristic impatience. "Where have you been, Blackhaw?"

"What's up?"

"I can't tell you over the phone. We need you here. Now."

Trevor gave directions to their location and ended the call. "There's some new development."

"About the Militia?"

"I suppose."

To be sure, Trevor cared if they were hot on the trail of Boone Fowler and his men, but it wasn't the first thing on his mind. He hoped it would wait until tomorrow.

He led her to a flat rock beside a pine tree, and they sat down. Again he gazed at the mine shaft. "We heard someone following."

"Deer Hunter," she said. "That's the Cherokee name for the man they called Snake. He killed the prison guard who whacked you."

"You saw this?"

She nodded. "Snapped his neck like a twig. Then Warden Green left him alone with us. He was supposed to murder us, too. And leave our bodies in the mine shaft so we would never be found."

A clever move on Green's part. Without their bodies, a police investigation would ultimately stall. "Why didn't Deer Hunter do as he was ordered?"

"Because you're a warrior. To kill you would disrespect your ancestors."

Nodding, Trevor accepted her explanation. Though Deer Hunter was on the other side of the law, there was a bond of blood between them. Trevor had felt it the first time he saw the dangerous man with the Cherokee tattoo. "He must have gotten lost in the labyrinth and followed us."

As they watched, the big man stepped out of the cave. Silently, he raised his arms to the sky, embracing his freedom. He glanced toward them, then walked in the opposite direction, disappearing into the shadows of the forest.

At another time, under other circumstances, Trevor might have pursued this escaped fugitive. But not today. *"Da-na-da-go-hv-i."* *Goodbye, my brother.*

BACK AT THE BOUNTY HUNTER headquarters, new developments had created a stir. All the men, except for Murphy, who was still recovering in the hospital, were there. With all of them poised for action, Sierra figured the testosterone level topped the chart. Before they started beating their chests and howling, she locked herself in the bathroom to take a shower.

The last time she'd bathed, Trevor had been with her. As she stood under the pulsing water, she closed her eyes and remembered his muscular arms wrapped around her. Was it possible to feel safe and sexy at the same time? He'd promised her a bedroom tonight.

Her eyelids snapped open. It wasn't likely that they'd have private time together. The bounty hunters were planning a complex maneuver. They'd received an anonymous phone call threatening their former Special Forces unit, stationed in North Carolina. Further intelligence confirmed that Special Forces was about to be deployed in a surgical strike against the Lukinberg terrorists.

The bounty hunters wanted to be there in the midst of the action. They wanted to mobilize, to go to the East Coast and thwart the attack against Special Forces. It was a matter of pride and loyalty—a code of honor that she could only understand in the context of Deer Hunter. Though he was a killer, he'd spared Trevor and her. His reasons had to do with brotherhood and the respect of one warrior for another.

She rinsed the shampoo from her hair and allowed

the steaming water to slide down her back. She could understand the code of honor, but she didn't like it.

If she had anything to say, Trevor would stay with her, safe in her arms. She'd come too close to losing him.

After she toweled dry and dressed in jeans and a clean T-shirt, she returned to the living room. Trevor pulled her forward. "Tell them what happened at the Fortress."

The eyes of all the bounty hunters were upon her. A less confident woman might have been intimidated, but Sierra was nothing if not mouthy. "First thing," she said, "Trevor used his interrogation techniques on Green. Very impressive. Green practically confessed that he'd arranged to have Lyle killed."

Trevor brushed off the compliment. "Tell them about the tunnel."

"Down in the lowest level of the Fortress is an area called the dungeon. Under one of the flagstones in the last cell is an escape tunnel that leads into an abandoned mine shaft. Green arranged for the Militia to escape that way."

"Remember the copper mine hideout we found?" Trevor asked. "It connects with the Fortress."

"How did the warden get involved with the Militia?" Mike asked. "He arranged their escape. Why?"

"For a payoff," Trevor said. "The warden runs on greed."

"But the Militia isn't well-funded," Mike said.

"Exactly right," Trevor said. "Somebody else is footing the bills. Somebody who also financed the attack on the Galleria. That's who we need to go after."

"Somebody who is using them," Mike said. "A mastermind."

"We need to know that person's identity," Trevor said. "We've got to talk to the warden."

"Later," Riley said as he rose to his feet. "That's something we can take care of after we get back from the East Coast."

"It can't wait," Trevor said. "Green's retirement starts today. He's flying out of here on a chartered plane. After that, he'll be gone. I want to go after him. Immediately."

"To interrogate him," Mike said. "You're the right man for that job, Blackhaw."

The other men exchanged glances, communicating without words. They all nodded.

"Get back here on the double," Riley said. "Several of us are deploying tonight… You included."

Trevor executed a sharp pivot and came toward her. He took her hand to lead her to the door.

"Wait a minute," she said as she grabbed her parka. "Okay, now I'm ready."

On the wide porch outside, he closed the door and turned to face her. The glow from the porch light shone on his rugged features, and she could see how tired he was. Gently, he said, "You're not coming with me."

"What do you mean?" She playfully shoved at his broad chest. "No way you're leaving me behind."

"This meeting with Green could get ugly. I won't deliberately take you into danger, Sierra. I want you to stay here at the headquarters, where you'll be safe."

"We're partners," she snapped. "If there's danger to you, I need to be there."

"Don't worry about me. I can handle Green. He'll be at his home—not at the prison, where he can call on his corrupt guards for help." He lightly touched her arm. "Give me a kiss, and I'll be back before you know it."

She stepped away from him. "Since when have I been cast in the role of sweet little woman who waits for her big strong man to take care of things?"

"You've always been a sweet woman."

"Bull!"

"Maybe a little rough around the edges, but—"

"If there's really no danger, why can't I come?"

He folded his arms across his chest and leaned against the log wall of the headquarters. "You've been through enough. Green tried to kill you. Perry Johnson stalked you. You were targeted at the Galleria."

"I can take it," she protested.

"Even before you met me," he said, "that bastard Lyle abused you and stole your money. You lost your unborn child—"

"Wait!" She had never said anything to him about her miscarriage. How did he know?

Chapter Fifteen

She was angry and confused. Sierra knew she'd never spoken to Trevor of the heart-wrenching sorrow she'd experienced when she lost her unborn son. Never had she said a word about that devastating pain. And yet he knew.

A vague memory took form in her mind. The interrogation room. Trevor standing over her, threatening her, manipulating her with the same kind of techniques he'd used so cleverly on Warden Green. And she'd wept bitter tears as she'd told him of her miscarriage.

Coldly, she glared at him. "You made me tell you. When I was tied up in that chair, you tricked me."

He said not one word to defend his reprehensible actions.

"You had no right," she said. "Against my will, you forced me to tell my secrets. Why didn't I remember until now?"

"I had hoped you never would remember."

"Did you drug me?"

He didn't need to answer. She saw the guilty truth in his eyes. He had drugged her! This just got worse and worse. "My God, Trevor. How can I ever trust you again?"

He recoiled as though she'd slapped him. "I'm sorry."

His apology came too late. If he'd told her earlier about the interrogation, she might have forgiven him. But to find out like this? When he was trying to use the tragedy of her miscarriage against her? "How could you?"

"It's my job," he said. "I'm an interrogator. That's what I do. And I had reason to suspect that you had information about the Militia."

"You had no reason. You went on a fishing expedition inside my brain, and you didn't care if you hurt me."

"I was wrong."

"Damn straight." She stomped down the porch steps and charged toward where the cars were parked. "Please give me a ride to my home."

He trailed behind her. "I think it's better if you stay here."

She whirled. "I don't give a damn what you think. I want to go home."

As she rode beside him in the car, her outrage simmered. He'd invaded her private life. Without her permission, he'd examined her deepest secret. Then he dared to claim that he was just doing his job. That sounded like the kind of thing Lyle used to say as an excuse for hanging around with the likes of Perry Johnson.

In her rational mind, she knew there was a world of difference between Lyle Nelson and Trevor Blackhaw. Trevor was trying to save the world. Lyle had wanted to destroy it. But they were both driven by loyalty to their peers and a need to do their job. Her concerns would always take second place.

When he pulled up at a stop sign, he turned to her. "This isn't over, Sierra."

"If you're referring to our relationship, you're wrong. It is so over."

"I won't give up."

"Forget it." She stared through the night at him. Why did he have to be so handsome? Why did his deep voice sound like a caress? "I never want to see you again."

"You mean everything to me," he said. "Everything."

"Then prove it," she said. "Come into my house and stay here with me instead of going to confront Warden Green."

Slowly, he pulled away from the stop sign. "You know I can't do that."

"You have a choice, Trevor."

"If I let Green get away, all our efforts will have been for nothing. Our escape through the tunnel. The safe deposit box. The showdown with Perry Johnson."

She understood how all those things pointed to this moment and the chance that Warden Green could reveal the name of the individual who had paid for the Militia's escape.

"I can't let them get away," Trevor declared. "Think of the Galleria. The people who died. Those who were injured."

"Of course I don't want the bad guys to escape," she said. "But why do you have to be the one who questions Green? Why not the police? The FBI?"

"Because I'm an interrogator," he replied. "And I'm the best."

He parked in front of her house, but didn't turn off the engine.

"Here we are, Trevor. Are you coming inside?"

"I can't."

"Just this once." She fought to keep the pleading tone from her voice. "Put my needs first."

The silence that stretched between them was deeper and more profound than the horrible darkness in the mine shaft. And even more foreboding. If he chose his work instead of her, their relationship was truly dead.

She opened her car door and climbed out. Though she tried to keep her head high, her shoulders were weighted by sadness. She'd been a fool to risk her heart again.

After unlocking her door, she stepped inside. Her duplex felt cold and empty.

"Damn you, Trevor." She went straight through to the kitchen and opened the refrigerator. There wasn't much inside. Worst of all, there was no ice cream in the freezer, nothing to ease her pain. "Why can't I catch a break?"

Still muttering, she closed the fridge door and stomped into the living room. "Trevor, you stubborn jerk. I never should have wasted one minute on you. How could you be so—"

She turned on the light.

Sitting in the middle of her sofa was Warden Craig Green. He held a gun in his hand. "Well, well," he said. "Sounds like there's trouble in paradise."

"What are you doing here?"

"I regularly listen to the police band radio. And I monitor other law enforcement, including the Big Sky Bounty Hunters." He rose from the sofa and came toward her. "Imagine my surprise when I heard Trevor asking to be picked up. He was supposed to be dead. And so were you."

Her gaze darted around the room. There had to be some way to protect herself—a way to escape. "I thought you were in a hurry to leave town."

"I can't very well leave you and your boyfriend alive," he said. "You know too much."

TREVOR DROVE TO THE END of her block and parked. Warden Green's house was only fifteen minutes away from here. He needed that time to prepare his strategy and to arm himself. Before leaving head-quarters, he hadn't taken the time to make sure he had the weaponry he might need, but Clark had been using this vehicle and he was a Beretta man.

In the glove compartment, Trevor found Clark's automatic and inserted the clip. This ought to be enough to convince the warden, who'd already shown himself to be weak and motivated only by a payoff.

Checking in the rear of the car, Trevor located a long-range rifle. Not necessary for this interroga-tion. With luck, Trevor wouldn't need guns at all. He had only one question for the warden: who paid you to free the Militia?

That name was the key. If the Militia's funds were cut off, they'd be forced to reveal themselves. They'd be easy prey. With that information, the end of this long search was in sight. Trevor should have been ex-hilarated, should have felt the pumping of adrenaline through his veins.

Instead, he felt empty inside. He missed her already.

A confrontation with Green—even a successful interrogation—was no solace. His heart told him to get out of the car and go back to her, to do whatever it took to earn her forgiveness. In the brief time they'd been together, she'd given him more than any other woman. She was meant to be with him. They were soul mates.

But he couldn't ignore his duty. There was a job

to be done, and he was the most skilled man to do it. If he walked away from this confrontation with Warden Green, Trevor could never live with himself.

And if he walked away from Sierra? His life wouldn't be worth living.

Though it went against his training and his instincts as a warrior, Trevor decided that somebody else would have to handle the interrogation of Warden Green. Sierra was more important. Right now he needed to put her first.

He opened his car door and strode down the street toward her house. At the front door, he paused before ringing the bell. There were voices coming from inside. Who was with her?

He eased to the edge of her porch and peeked through the window. What he saw turned his blood to ice water. Warden Green held a gun on Sierra. He stood right beside her with the bore of his pistol pressed against her temple. Even if Trevor could take a clear shot at Green, the warden might squeeze the trigger in reflex. And Sierra would pay the price.

"Call him," Green demanded. "Call your half-breed boyfriend and tell him that you want him to come here to your welcoming arms."

"I'd have to be pretty dumb to do that. As soon as he walks through the door, you're going to shoot him. And then you'll kill me. What do I get out of this?"

"You're in no position to bargain, my dear." He pushed his weapon against her head. "I have the gun."

"But it won't do you any good to kill me if Trevor is still alive. He knows everything I do."

Outside her window, Trevor shuddered. She was playing games with a desperate man.

"There are so many ways to die," Green said. "In my years at the Fortress, I've learned how to break a man's spirit. You have no idea how much pain I can inflict."

"You don't scare me."

"Then you're a fool."

Trevor had an idea. He took out his cell phone and dialed her number.

Inside the house, her telephone rang.

"Don't answer," Green snapped.

Quickly Trevor moved out of earshot. He waited until her answering machine beeped. Knowing his words would be broadcast into her living room, he said, "Sierra, this is Trevor. I went to Green's house, but he's already left. I'm going to the airfield to stop him. Meet me there. I have something special, and I need to give it to you in person." Trying to give her a clue, he added, "Drive carefully, partner. Don't go too fast."

He disconnected the call and edged back to the window with his gun ready. If Green tried to kill

Sierra before leaving, Trevor had no choice but to shoot right now. That was a dangerous solution. He hoped the warden would grab the bait and take Sierra to the airfield.

She reached for her parka. Green prodded her toward the door with his pistol. As they walked outside, Trevor ducked around the side of the house.

When they pulled away from the curb, with Sierra behind the wheel, he sprinted to his vehicle, which was still parked at the end of the street. It was imperative for him to arrive at the private airfield outside Ponderosa before they did. He needed time to plan his ambush.

Driving hard and fast, he raced through the sleepy streets, taking every shortcut he knew. Sierra's life depended on his swift action. Even if she drove at half speed, he'd have only minutes to spare.

Trevor knew he'd arrived first. With an expert eye he scanned the terrain, measuring the distance from the thick tree, and bushes to the parking area. Years of experience in combat told him exactly where to set up.

He hid the car, grabbed his long-range rifle and dashed across the open land until he found his vantage point. Then he waited.

With an effort, he controlled his unsteady breathing and calmed his pulse rate. Though he was an expert marksman, it had been a long time since he'd used his skill as a sniper. He couldn't fail. Sierra's life hung in the balance.

As he watched, Green's car chugged into the parking lot. When Sierra emerged from the driver's side, her head swiveled, and he knew she was scanning the area, looking for him, looking for her chance to escape. She leaned forward. He could tell that she intended to run.

Silently he prayed. *No, Sierra. Don't tempt him. Don't make a move.*

Green came around the back of the car. His arm was low as he tried to hide the handgun he had trained on her.

Trevor peered through the nightscope on the rifle. He had the warden in his sight. If he shot Green in the arm, the man would still be able to talk. Trevor might still get the necessary information.

He watched as Sierra started talking to Green again. She moved, inadvertently blocking Trevor's vision. *Damn it, Sierra. Settle down. Don't provoke him.*

She shoved at Green's chest. While he was momentarily off balance, she started running, heading toward the brushy area where Trevor hid.

He saw Green raise his handgun and aim. He meant to shoot her in the back.

Trevor fired first. It was a direct hit. With one bullet, he brought the warden down.

It was over. She was safe.

Tossing his rifle aside, Trevor stepped into the open. "Sierra."

Her long legs churned as she dashed toward him at full tilt, not slowing until she was in his arms.

"You're safe now," he said.

"Good work, partner."

Their lips joined, and he knew that he'd made the right choice in protecting her. She came first. She was more important than anything else.

The fullness of her body aroused him, and he was surprised that he could transform from sniper to lover in a matter of seconds. He wanted her with all his heart and soul.

Unfortunately, now was not the time for anything more than a quick kiss. A security guard at the airfield had reacted to the gunfire and was standing at Green's body, pointing his handgun in their direction. He yelled, "Put your hands up. Do it now."

Trevor stepped away from Sierra and obeyed. "Better do what he says."

She nodded. "After all we've been through, I don't want to get shot by a security guard."

Side by side, with their hands raised, they walked toward the gun-waving guard.

"Do you think Green is going to survive?" she asked.

"Only with a miracle." Trevor was pretty sure he'd drilled the warden in the center of his chest.

"I'm sorry," she said. "You didn't get the information you needed."

He looked down at the beautiful woman who walked beside him. "You're all I need."

Her smile rewarded him. "That phone call you made to my house. You were giving me a message, right? When you told me to drive slow?"

"I was standing outside your window."

"You never went to interrogate Green," she said. "You came back to me."

"You come first, Sierra."

SIERRA WAS GLAD that his promise to put her first had not been tested by the plans of the other bounty hunters. After killing the warden, Trevor had gone through several hours of questioning by the local sheriff and the FBI. He was unable to join his comrades, who had deployed to North Carolina to rescue their former platoon.

That was two days ago. Two glorious days. She and Trevor had flown to a ski resort and taken a suite with a hot tub, where they were spending much of their time naked. Bobbing in the heated water, she closed her eyes and allowed the pulsating jets to massage her. Behind her eyelids she imagined the strong, handsome man who sat across from her in the tub. His broad shoulders. His long black hair. His incredible blue eyes.

She waited for a moment until her internal vision

of him was completely formed. Her anticipation built. She was like a kid at Christmas, dreaming of her first bicycle waiting under the tree.

Then she opened her eyes, and there he was— even better than she'd imagined.

"You look worried," she said. "Thinking about the guys?"

"I haven't heard from them in a while."

"They've probably got their hands full. Fighting evil and all." She reached for her champagne glass and took a sip. "I'm sure they'll be okay."

"I keep thinking about that anonymous phone call telling them that the platoon would come under attack. It seemed like a setup."

"Like at the Galleria, when the Militia used hostages to lure all the law enforcement guys, then detonated their nerve gas." Thinking of that assault reminded her of something else. "How's Cameron doing?"

"He's got some nerve damage, but he ought to recover. Can't wait to get out of the hospital."

"You know what they say." She glided through the bubbling water toward him. "It's hard to keep a good man down."

Though he kissed her when she reached him, she could tell he was still preoccupied, worried about his friends, who might be walking into a trap. No matter how much she wished he could stay with her forever, that was not to be. In his heart, Trevor would always be a warrior. And, she realized, that was one of the things she loved about him.

Hoping to distract him, she reached for the remote and turned on the television. "Yuck, it's the news."

"Leave it on that channel," he said. "Might be good to catch up on what's happening in the rest of the world."

She rubbed against him, blissfully familiar with his incredible naked body. "I wanted to ask you something. Remember when you called my house? When Green was there?"

"Yeah?"

"You said you had a surprise for me. What was it?"

"I've been waiting for the right moment," he said.

"Now," she said firmly. "Life's too short to wait. The right moment is now."

He maneuvered until he was facing her. The bubbling water of the hot tub swirled around his chest. He pulled the silver ring from his finger— the ring with the seven-pointed Cherokee star. "With this token, I pledge my devotion. I will never lie to you or conceal the truth. Our bond will last for all eternity."

Her mouth gaped. She was speechless.

"Marry me, Sierra. I love you with all my heart."

"Yes."

He placed the ring on her finger. "I want babies. Lots of babies."

Happiness overwhelmed her. She threw her arms

around him and held on tightly. "Oh, yes. I love you, Trevor."

Their embrace and their kisses were obviously leading somewhere else, and they rose from the hot tub. It was only a few steps to the bed, but he was distracted by the television. Crown Prince Nikolai was denouncing the Militia, calling them terrorists.

Sierra grabbed the remote. "I'm getting real tired of this guy."

"Wait." Trevor held her hand.

In front of the TV camera, Nikolai was defying his father, King Aleksandr. "…And I will use whatever resources are at my disposal to assist in the safe return of America's heroic hostages."

"What hostages?" Trevor demanded.

His cell phone rang, and Sierra grabbed it. For a moment she was tempted to throw the phone into the hot tub and avoid what she feared would be bad news.

But she couldn't stop Trevor from being who he was: strong, heroic and brave.

When she answered, she immediately recognized the voice of Trevor's former commander. "Hello, Cameron."

"Bad news," he said. "Four of the bounty hunters have been taken hostage along with the Special Forces platoon."

She glanced toward Trevor, her newly betrothed. "Let me guess. You need Trevor's help to rescue them."

"I need to talk to him."

"One minute." She gazed into the blue eyes of the man she loved. It would be hard to let him go, but she couldn't force him to stay. She held the phone to her breast. "Promise that you'll come back to me."

"Always. Sierra, you are my life."

She hoped their life together would last for a very long time, until they were both old and gray, with grandchildren playing around their feet. But she couldn't force him not to take risks. That was what he did. Luckily, he was damn good at it.

"Go for it." She handed him the phone. "Do what you have to do."

Before turning his attention to his new mission, Trevor sealed his promise to Sierra with a kiss neither would ever forget.

* * * * *

Don't miss the continuation of
BIG SKY BOUNTY HUNTERS,
when Julie Miller tells battle-scarred Bryce Martin's story in Forbidden Captor,
coming next month from Intrigue!

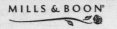

FREE!
4 Books
and a surprise gift!

We would like to take this opportunity to thank you for reading this Mills & Boon® book by offering you the chance to take FOUR more specially selected titles from the Intrigue™ series absolutely FREE! We're also making this offer to introduce you to the benefits of the Mills & Boon® Reader Service™—

- ★ FREE home delivery
- ★ FREE gifts and competitions
- ★ FREE monthly Newsletter
- ★ Exclusive Reader Service offers
- ★ Books available before they're in the shops

Accepting these FREE books and gift places you under no obligation to buy. you may cancel at any time. even after receiving your free shipment. Simply complete your details below and return the entire page to the address below. You don't even need a stamp!

YES! Please send me 4 free Intrigue books and a surprise gift. I understand that unless you hear from me. I will receive 6 superb new titles every month for just £3.10 each. postage and packing free. I am under no obligation to purchase any books and may cancel my subscription at any time. The free books and gift will be mine to keep in any case.

17ZEF

Ms/Mrs/Miss/Mr ....Initials ....
                                                        BLOCK CAPITALS PLEASE
Surname ....
Address ....

....

....Postcode ....

Send this whole page to:
UK: FREEPOST CN81, Croydon, CR9 3WZ